The girls made their way back to their hotel room. As Cassie opened the door of the room, a prickly feeling in her scalp told her that something wasn't quite right, even before she looked in.

'Wait here, a minute,' she whispered to Becky and Poppy.

Cassie edged cautiously into the room and gave a little squeal. Becky and Poppy dashed in after her and gasped.

The girls' beautiful costumes for their *Cinderella* ballet were strewn all over the floor, along with their quilts and pillows. Splashed over them, and over the pale carpet, were several large black ink-blots.

'Who could have done this?' Cassie cried in horror.

The Ballet School series

On Tour with the Ballet School

Mal Lewis Jones

Hodder
Children's
Books

a division of Hodder Headline plc

Children for cover illustration courtesy of Gaston Payne School
of Theatre, Dance and Drama.
Special thanks to Freed of London Ltd., 94 St Martins Lane,
London WC2N for the loan of dancewear

First published in Great Britain in 1995
by Hodder Children's Books

10 9 8 7 6 5 4 3 2

A Catalogue record for this book is available from the British Library

ISBN 0 340 60733 5

Typeset by Avon Dataset Ltd, Bidford-on-Avon

Printed and bound in Great Britain by
Cox & Wyman Ltd, Reading, Berks.

Hodder Children's Books
A Division of Hodder Headline plc
338 Euston Road
London NW1 3BH

Contents

For my son, Levin

1

Dover to Calais

'Come on, Dad!' screeched Cassandra Brown from the back seat of the car. 'We're going to miss the coach!'

'Don't panic, Cassie,' said her father, Jake. 'If they said to get to school for midnight, it's bound to be twelve-thirty or so before the coach actually leaves.'

'But can't we go faster?' urged Cassie.

'No,' said Jake firmly. 'We're going quite fast enough for the road conditions.'

An unseasonable frost had left the roads icy and dangerous. Jake Brown was taking no chances, especially on the stretch of motorway which was leading them closer to the outskirts of England's second city.

'They'll wait for us!' he continued.

'Not if we're too late,' said Cassie impatiently.

As they left the motorway, Cassie again checked the clock on the car's dashboard. Ten past twelve. It was unthinkable that she might miss the coach from Redwood Ballet School, the coach which was to take her and her friends to France for a magical week's performance tour.

'Oh please hurry, Dad,' she pleaded.

'I'll get you there, don't worry,' he replied. 'And what's more, all in one piece. Now don't forget what your mother said about eating plenty and remembering your inhalers.'

'Don't fuss, Dad,' Cassie answered. With a flick of her head, she tossed her dark brown hair out of her equally dark brown eyes and thrust her chin forward. Jake knew the gesture well – it meant Cassie wasn't going to budge. 'Just keep your mind on your driving!'

In another ten minutes they were chugging down the long drive to Redwood. Their headlights swept across several orderly lines of parked cars and finally illuminated a coach full of waving youngsters. It was pulled up outside the large Georgian school buildings.

As Cassie tore open the passenger door, the uplifting sound of cheering met her ears. Jake helped her with her luggage.

'I must be the last!' she said.

'Well, they didn't go without you, did they? Now, we'll be expecting a call on Tuesday, don't forget!'

Cassie grinned at her dad and kissed him goodbye, before joining her noisy friends on the coach. She wasn't likely to forget to ring home on Tuesday. Tuesday would be her thirteenth birthday – the first birthday she had ever spent away from her family, falling as it always did in the Easter holidays.

'We're very relieved to see you,' said Miss Oakland, register in hand. 'We shouldn't have liked to be without our Spring Fairy!'

Miss Oakland, their ballet teacher, appeared to be in a good mood for a change.

'No, Miss Oakland. Sorry I'm a bit late.'

Madame Larette, the principal ballet mistress, also greeted her as she moved down the coach towards her friends, Becky and Poppy, who were waving frantically at her. They'd saved her a seat beside them.

'I thought you weren't going to make it!' Becky exclaimed.

'You're not the only one!' laughed Cassie.

They all felt terribly excited about this trip to France. Even though it was way past everyone's bedtime, for the first part of the coach journey sleep was out of the question.

'I can't wait to see the Eiffel Tower!' cried Poppy.

'Well, you'll have to,' said Becky. 'We're not going to Paris until Tuesday.'

3

'My birthday in Paris . . .' said Cassie dreamily.

'Oops,' said Becky. 'I'd forgotten all about it. Never mind, I'm sure I'll be able to get you a pressie over there.'

'Yes, what would you like?' asked Poppy.

Cassie paused to think. 'I wouldn't mind a new teddy.'

'But, Cassie, you've got dozens of soft toys already!' Becky remonstrated.

Cassie grinned. 'I like them,' she said. Then her expression grew sad as she remembered taking Little Ted into hospital last term to leave with their friend Emily, who had suffered from anorexia nervosa.

'It seems awful that Emily's not here with us,' she said with a sigh.

'Well at least she's getting better,' said Becky sensibly. 'The way things were going last term I wondered if she was ever going to make it back to school.'

'Yes,' agreed Cassie. 'I'm sure spending the holidays with her family all together again will put her right back on her feet.'

'Has her dad gone back home then?' asked Poppy.

'At weekends for now. And when they can sell their house, they're all moving down to Birmingham.'

As the girls went on chattering about Emily and all that had happened before Easter, they failed to notice their school-mates dropping off to sleep around them. At about half past one Miss Oakland glided down the coach with a warning frown.

'Stop talking now,' she whispered, 'and get some sleep. You'll be glad of it tomorrow.'

The girls had little option but to take her advice. Cassie didn't wake until the coach came to a standstill, waiting in the queue to board the ferry at Dover. She was surprised to find most of the other students wide awake. Matthew and Tom came forward from the back seat and, before Cassie could stop them, tickled a snoring Becky in the ribs.

'Get off!' Becky exploded as she woke instantly.

Poppy was stirring too. 'Oh, I might have known it would be you two!' she said.

'Oh my gawd!' said Tom in mock horror, pointing at Poppy's head. 'What's that in your hair?'

Poppy squealed despite herself, shaking a black rubber spider free of her red mop.

'Oh, get lost,' she said. 'I've only just woken up.'

The boys went back to their seats laughing.

'I hope they're not going to be like this all week,' said Cassie.

The students were all glad to stretch their legs as they spilled off the coach and made their way to the below-deck accommodation of the ferry. Cassie and her friends paused to buy some sweets and drinks.

'Look over there!' said Becky. 'Those three are in trouble already.'

Mr Whistler, the tap teacher who was in charge of the boys on the trip, was talking earnestly to Matthew, Tom and Ojo. The boys were looking decidedly sheepish.

5

'Oh, isn't it great being at sea!' Cassie exclaimed flinging her arms wide and knocking a can of coke all over Celia, who had just come up behind them.

'Oh sorry, Celia!' Cassie said. She took out a tissue and started dabbing it at the other girl's jumper.

'Leave it alone!' Celia snapped. 'You'll make it ten times worse. Trust you to do something like this.'

Cassie's remorse swiftly changed to irritation. 'Well, if you hadn't come sneaking up behind me, it would never have happened!' she retorted.

'Come on, Cassie,' Becky urged. 'You were just telling me how much fun it was being here!'

Taking the hint, Cassie followed Becky and Poppy down a walkway. The boat was starting to roll now and they found it difficult keeping their balance as they moved forwards. After a few minutes of exploring, Becky announced that she was feeling sea-sick.

'You do look pale,' Cassie agreed.

'I'm always pale,' said Becky.

'No, but paler than usual,' said Cassie. Indeed, Becky's skin had almost turned the colour of her white-blonde hair.

'You'd be better up on deck,' Poppy suggested. So the three girls climbed up into the fresh air. A cool breeze chilled them immediately, but Becky was revived by the air and spray on her face. They were delighted by the dawn breaking in pink streaks over the sea.

'I wish I were a painter,' Cassie said dreamily. 'Then I could capture those lovely colours and shapes.'

'No you don't,' said Becky. 'You wish you were a dancer. Remember?'

'I was joking,' laughed Cassie. Dancing had always been her one and only ambition.

'Are you looking forward to our first performance tomorrow night?' asked Poppy who had been gazing out to sea. 'I'm starting to feel nervous.'

'You'll be fine, Poppy,' said Cassie. 'You'll make a wonderful Fairy Godmother.'

'It's a pity you're not dancing Cinderella,' said Poppy. 'You probably would have been if it hadn't been for your asthma attacks last term.'

Cassie shrugged. 'Well, we'll never know now. Anyway, I'm not going to lose any sleep over it. I've got a good solo, which is tons better than just being in the corps de ballet. And I've had chance to understudy the part of Cinderella. And after all, I'm here, that's the main thing.'

'Yes,' said Becky. 'Thank goodness you got better in time.'

At that moment, Celia and Abigail joined them on deck.

'It's a bit bracing up here, isn't it?' said Abi, shivering.

'Not so sick-making though,' countered Becky.

'Come on, Abi,' said Celia, 'let's go back below deck. You might catch a chill and think how awful that would be. We wouldn't have a Cinderella.' She glanced spitefully at Cassie. 'At least not a decent one!'

Before Cassie could make a retort, Celia had whisked Abigail out of earshot.

'Pity you knocked that coke over Celia,' said Becky when they'd disappeared.

'It was an accident!'

'I know, but you shouldn't have lost your temper with her. You know what she's like. She might do something stupid. Just to get back at you.'

'Oh, I don't care,' said Cassie, shrugging. 'She doesn't bother me. She's been a bit better since Abi took her under her wing.'

'It's no good my giving you advice,' Poppy chipped in. 'I always have a nearly-uncontrollable urge to blow my top every time she comes anywhere near me.'

The sky lightened as they drew into Calais. With very little delay, the students were back in the coach, steaming along to their first destination, Amiens, where they were to spend two nights.

'Thank goodness we're not dancing tonight!' Cassie exclaimed after a jaw-cracking yawn. 'I'm exhausted.'

'So am I,' said Becky, 'and I still feel queasy.'

'I wonder what lunch will be like at the hotel,' said Poppy.

'Oh don't,' Becky winced.

Their first impressions of Amiens were watery

ones. The Somme river cut through the middle and they could see masses of market gardens criss-crossed with water channels and larger canals, forming lakes and islands, draped with willows and poplars.

They drove past an ancient cathedral, through a shopping centre, to their hotel, which was in a more run-down part of the town.

'Belle Vue!' exclaimed Becky, pointing to the name of the building. 'They've got a vivid imagination.'

The hotel actually over-looked some very dilapidated warehouses.

'I don't care what the view's like,' said Poppy, 'as long as the food's good.'

But the girls were to be disappointed. They were shown to their twin rooms – Cassie and Becky in one, Poppy and Rhiannon, who was dancing the part of the Autumn Fairy alongside Cassie, next door. Then they unpacked their luggage and found their way to the restaurant for lunch.

Presented with some very greasy, watery soup, Becky complained of not feeling at all hungry. She went off to sit in the lounge by herself.

'That's not at all like Becky,' said Cassie.

'She's not missing much,' said Poppy. 'This soup's awful. I'd give better to a pig.'

Cassie looked round the restaurant. There were disgruntled faces all about her. Even the teachers seemed to be eating very little.

'What a pity we're here for two days,' whispered Cassie.

'What are we supposed to do with ourselves this afternoon?' Poppy asked.

'We're going sightseeing round Amiens,' Cassie replied.

'Pity I didn't bring my wellies,' said Poppy gloomily. 'There seems to be water everywhere!'

Cassie smiled. 'I saw some boats on the river. We could go for a boat trip.'

Poppy's face brightened. 'That's a brilliant idea. But perhaps it's not quite the right time to mention it to Becky.'

The girls went to join Becky in the lounge.

'How are you feeling?' Cassie asked.

'I don't feel so sick,' Becky answered, 'but when I walk around, I still feel as if the floor's rolling and rocking beneath my feet.'

'You don't feel like a stroll round the hotel?'

'No thanks,' groaned Becky.

'OK then,' said Cassie. She turned to Poppy. 'Do you want to come back to our room?'

'Yes, that would be nice. Just for a bit. What time have we got to meet Madame in the lounge?'

'Not for an hour yet.'

'Fine,' said Poppy. 'I'll have time to sort out my costume. It's looking a bit crushed; has anyone brought an iron?'

'Yes, I think Miss Oakland said she was bringing a travel iron,' Becky answered.

The girls carried on down the corridor, slowly, so as not to make Becky feel worse. But as Cassie

10

opened the door of their room, a prickly feeling in her scalp told her that something wasn't quite right even before she looked in. She edged cautiously into the room and gave a little squeal. Becky and Poppy dashed in after her and gasped.

The girls' costumes were strewn all over the floor, along with their quilts and pillows. Splashed over them, *and* over the pale-coloured carpet, were several large black ink-blots.

2

A French Teddy

'Who could have done this?' Cassie cried in horror.

'And what will we dance in tomorrow?' Poppy exclaimed.

'Hold on,' said Becky, her sickness forgotten. 'I think someone's been playing a practical joke.'

She picked up her ugly sister costume and the ink blot fell off onto the floor. It was a paper cut-out. Cassie and Poppy flew to their own costumes and to their great relief found that the blots on them were also fake.

'Someone must have spilled some black ink on a piece of paper and then cut out blot shapes,' said Cassie, examining hers.

'I wonder who?' said Poppy.

'Perhaps it was Celia, trying to get revenge,' suggested Becky.

'We'll tackle her this afternoon,' said Poppy.

'No, we won't,' said Cassie thoughtfully.

'Let's not give her the pleasure of knowing we were taken in.'

'Good idea,' Becky agreed. 'She'll probably end up admitting it, just to find out what our reaction was.'

After tidying up the room, the girls went down to the lounge to meet Madame Larette and the other students. They were put in Madame Larette's own group and set off into the centre of Amiens on foot. Cassie was glad to be in Madame's group because she knew such a lot about the history of the place. Madame explained that Amiens was the ancient capital of the region called Picardy. She made the thirteenth century cathedral their first stop. It was one of the largest in France. Inside the cathedral, Cassie was impressed by the height of the vaulted ceiling and the number of pillars; there must have been over a hundred. Madame pointed out the beautiful carving on the wooden choirstalls.

'There are four thousand figures carved into the choirstalls altogether,' said Madame.

'Wow,' whispered Becky. 'It must have taken them ages to do that.'

'And now we come to the rose window,' said Madame, leading them across to a beautiful stained-glass window.

14

As they moved across, Celia came to stand beside Becky.

'Done all your unpacking?' Becky couldn't resist asking her.

'Yes, I have actually,' Celia answered, 'and I've tried to get the coke stain out of my jumper, but it won't come out!'

She gave Cassie a dirty look. Despite her previous resolve to remain quiet on the subject, Cassie couldn't resist saying something heated in response.

'It was an accident, Celia. A bit different from going into someone's room and deliberately trying to upset them.'

'What are you talking about?' Celia said, raising her voice.

'Shh, Celia,' warned Abigail. 'Madame's coming this way.'

'Celia,' said Madame, 'you are in a house of prayer. Keep your voice down, s'il vous plait.'

'Sorry, Madame,' Celia muttered.

As she went off with Abigail to look at a tomb, Celia cast an angry glance at Cassie.

'Oh dear,' said Becky, 'not quite what we'd planned. Do you still think she did it?'

'I'm sure it was Celia,' replied Cassie. 'You know how easily she plays the innocent.'

The students eventually emerged from the west porch, where the tall, stone figures of early bishops guarded the entrance. They moved down to a little square. Enticing smells wafted from several shops, cafés and open stalls.

'Yummy,' said Becky, sniffing the air. 'I suddenly feel hungry.'

Most of the other students in the group joined Becky, Cassie and Poppy in the queue for hot croissants. The delicious croissants made up for their inadequate lunch.

Becky had finished hers long before anyone else. 'May I go into the sweet shop?' she asked Madame.

'Don't make yourself sick.'

'No, I'm making myself feel better,' said Becky grinning. As she went into the shop to buy chocolates and macarons d'Amiens, Cassie spotted some postcards on display outside the gift shop next door.

'I'd like to get a postcard for Emily,' she said to Poppy.

'OK,' said Poppy, still munching the last of her croissants. 'I'll tell Becky where you are and wait out here for you.'

It took a few seconds for Cassie's eyes to adjust to the dimly-lit interior of the shop after the bright sunshine outside. In fact, before she could see anything clearly in the cluttered shop, she was conscious of raised voices. Angry voices, speaking in French of course; Cassie couldn't understand a word. She squeezed her eyes shut and opened them again.

A door was open at the back of the shop and she could make out two men arguing in the room behind. One wore a navy and white striped, cotton jumper and a navy beret. The other man was dressed in a shirt and tie and smart, dark trousers.

Becky slipped into the shop and stood beside her.

'What's going on?' she whispered.

The men broke off their argument, noticing the girls for the first time. The smartly-dressed man shut the door firmly. As he did so, Cassie noticed a scar running across his cheek from the corner of his mouth, almost to the base of his ear. Shivering a little, she turned to Becky.

'I wonder what that was all about?'

A young woman appeared from another doorway behind the counter.

'Bonjour,' she said cheerfully.

'Bonjour,' Cassie repeated, self-consciously.

The woman placed a teddy-bear she'd been carrying on the counter and fluffed up its yellow ears.

'Oh, he's lovely,' Cassie said, as she gave the assistant the postcard she'd chosen. 'I mean, "Il est très joli." '

The young woman laughed and pushed the teddy-bear across the counter towards her.

'Voilà. He is old stock. I found him in the back room.' She pointed over her shoulder. Cassie was relieved she could speak English.

'I thought we 'ad sold all these teddies last year,' the young woman went on. 'He is très charmant, n'est-ce-pas?'

'Yes,' agreed Cassie. 'How much is he?'

'Oh, they used to be fifty francs, I think, but you

can 'ave him for twenty-five if you like.'

Impulsively, Cassie reached into her purse. Twenty-five francs would make a hole in her pocket money. But she had fallen in love with the bright yellow teddy-bear. She just had to buy him.

'Merci,' said Cassie, clutching her new acquisition proudly.

Becky had been browsing round the shop. Her eye was caught by a colourful box on a high shelf behind the counter.

'What's that?' she asked the assistant.

The young woman had to climb on a stool to reach the box.

'I don't know,' she admitted, as she brought it down. 'Ah, it's a money-box.'

Becky examined it. There was a slot on the top for coins to go in and a window at the front, revealing a shiny ball, which seemed to be suspended in mid-air.

'How extraordinary!' said Becky.

'Can I put a coin in and see what happens?' Becky asked.

'Oui,' said the woman, shrugging.

Becky dropped in an English penny. It vanished into the box.

'Ooh, that's clever,' said Cassie.

The woman laughed. 'It works with trick mirrors,' she explained.

'Are you going to buy it?' Cassie asked Becky.

'Of course. It's got my one pence inside!'

As the girls came out of the shop, they collided

with Madame Larette, who was rounding everyone up for the next stage of their sightseeing tour.

Just across from the cathedral was the river.

'I thought we'd take a punt trip,' said Madame, leading her group down river for a little way to the canal bank. Some flat-bottomed punts were available for hire.

'It'll take about an hour,' said Madame, 'and we'll go through the Hortillonages.'

'What are they?' asked Poppy.

'The waterlands – canals and lakes.'

'We saw them from the coach, didn't we?' asked Cassie.

'Ah, oui,' replied Madame.

She collected their fares and paid them to the man hiring out the punt.

''As anyone done this before?' she asked.

Matthew, Tom and a couple of the girls put their hands up. Matthew was assigned to Cassie's punt.

'Mind what you're doing with that pole,' called Poppy, as they got under way.

'Look, do you like my new teddy-bear?' asked Cassie, unwrapping him to show her friends.

'Oh, he's cute,' said Poppy. 'But I thought Becky was supposed to be buying you one for your birthday!'

'Oh, I wouldn't mind another one,' said Cassie. 'It was weird in the shop. There were two French men shouting at each other. One of them had a horrible scar across his cheek. It really gave me the creeps.'

'Matthew,' said Becky. 'Why are we going round in circles?'

The punt was indeed spinning slowly and all the other punts had moved ahead of them.

'Are you sure you've done this before?' asked Cassie suspiciously.

'No I haven't really,' Matthew admitted. 'I just fancied having a go.'

'Let me have the pole,' cried Cassie crossly. In no time at all, their punt was moving along quite nicely in the water. 'There,' she said. 'It takes skill.'

Matthew looked as though he were sulking. 'I'd have got the hang of it if you'd given me a chance,' he complained.

'Sorry, I'm enjoying myself now,' said Cassie.

'I suppose you're getting your own back,' Matthew muttered.

'What for?' asked Cassie in surprise.

It was Matthew's turn to look surprised.

'Oh – oh nothing,' he said quickly.

Cassie looked at Becky. *Is she thinking what I'm thinking?* she wondered.

'No, go on, Matthew,' said Cassie, leaning on the pole. 'Why should I be getting my own back?'

Matthew blushed under her inquisitorial gaze.

'I thought you'd guess it was us,' he said sheepishly.

'The ink-blots!' cried Poppy, suddenly putting two and two together.

'Sorry,' said Matthew. 'I've got this book see, called *Crazy Practical Jokes*, and . . .'

'Say no more,' said Cassie sternly. 'Just don't play another single trick on us or you're for it.'

'OK, OK. I get the message.'

'Cross your heart?'

'Cross my heart.'

'So it wasn't Celia after all,' said Cassie.

She felt a flush of guilt for accusing Celia wrongly. *It just shows you shouldn't jump to conclusions*, she thought to herself.

'Mmm. Anyone want a chocolate?' asked Becky, handing round the bag.

'I thought you got sea-sick, Becky,' said Matthew.

'Since when has a canal had waves, you idiot,' said Becky. 'I could sit here for hours.'

'You'll probably have to, if Cassie gets any nearer to the bank,' said Matthew. 'It looks muddy and much shallower just there.'

Cassie adjusted her course and glanced over her shoulder. Her heart skipped a beat. In a punt not far behind were two men, one in a beret, the other in a shirt and tie.

'Don't look now,' she whispered, 'but the two men from that gift shop are just behind us.'

'What a strange coincidence,' Poppy remarked. 'Are you sure it's the same men?'

'Well they're dressed the same,' agreed Becky.

'They look a nasty pair,' hissed Matthew.

'They didn't look too nice in the shop,' said Cassie. 'Does anyone want to take the pole? I'm tired now and I reckon we ought to catch up with the others.'

As Becky manned the pole, Cassie had a better look at the men. They seemed to be looking towards the children's punt. The man in shirt-sleeves had got a scar. She could see it now quite clearly.

'They're making the same mistake you did,' whispered Matthew. 'They're going too close to the bank. I can see a dark patch of weeds as well as mud.'

As Matthew had warned, the men's punt became stuck in the soft mud.

Cassie looked back. Both men were now standing in the punt, holding the pole and trying to lever themselves away from the bank. The vessel suddenly and unexpectedly came free and the men fell into the muddy water.

'Will they be all right, do you think?' asked Poppy.

'I don't fancy going back to help them,' said Cassie.

'They won't come to any harm,' said Matthew. 'The water there is really shallow.'

As they caught up with the rest of their party, the children watched the two men clamber up onto the bank; their punt was too far away now to reach.

'Can't say I'm sorry they didn't get any closer,' said Cassie.

'No, they didn't look too friendly,' Becky agreed.

'Look, we're almost back where we started,' Poppy said.

The children recognised the market gardens they had passed before, the black soil spotted with cauliflowers, cabbages and spring flowers.

Within another few minutes, the cathedral had

come back into view and they were pulling up with all the other punts.

The two men had run along the other side of the bank and were now level with the children. They looked a sorry sight: their clothes were muddy and dripping wet and a few brownish green weeds dangled from their hair. There was nowhere for them to cross the water. They started shouting at the lad in charge of the boats, and he shouted back in reply.

'What was all that about?' Cassie asked Madame, as the men ran further along the bank. 'The young man told them they'd have to go to the next lock, about a kilometre away,' Madame explained.

Somehow Cassie felt very glad that she and her friends would be safely back at the Belle Vue hotel before the men could return to the landing-stage.

'Alors, have we got everybody?' asked Madame, counting heads.

Matthew scurried back to Tom, anxious that Cassie might take him to task again for the ink-blot trick. He needn't have worried, however, for that had gone out of her mind. The image of the scar-faced man had obliterated it completely.

3

Feather Trouble

Cassie was making herself comfortable for the night.

'Oh, wait a minute,' she said to Becky, who was about to turn out the light. 'I've forgotten New Teddy.'

There was already a scruffy old teddy and a fat pink hippo in bed with her.

'Is that what you're going to call him?' asked Becky. 'New Teddy?'

'No, he ought to have a proper name. What do you think? Something French . . .'

'Pierre?'

'No, I've got it,' said Cassie enthusiastically.

'Edouard. He can be Teddy Edouard!'

'Are you ready now?' asked Becky, finger on the light switch.

'Yes, you can switch it off.'

Redwood rules were in force even while the children were in France. On evenings when they weren't performing, they were expected to be in bed at eight-thirty.

But on this particular Saturday night, Cassie and Becky found it impossible to settle down to sleep. Such a lot had happened in the previous twenty-four hours, and they felt excited at being in a strange place. They chattered about the day's happenings for so long that finally Miss Oakland arrived at their door, telling them to go straight to sleep, or there'd be trouble.

Cassie slept fitfully through the night, half-aware that she was wheezing, but too tired to sit up and do anything about it. By morning she had developed a full-blown asthma attack. Her inhalers could only relieve her a little.

'What do you think's caused this?' Becky asked, in concern, when she woke up. 'I mean, they won't have had any animals in here, will they?'

Cassie's asthma had been triggered the previous term by Becky bringing her hamster to stay in their bedroom.

'No,' coughed Cassie. 'I'm trying to remember what else the doctor said I was allergic to. Dust maybe?'

Becky looked round the room. Though very

simply furnished, there was not a speck of dirt anywhere. She shook her head.

'Try and remember what else he said.'

'Feathers,' Cassie replied, 'but I don't see any birds.'

'They don't have to be on birds, silly,' said Becky. 'What about your pillow?'

Cassie felt the pillow behind her back. 'It could be. It's very soft.'

Becky bounced over to Cassie's bed, her long, fair hair swishing forward over her shoulders.

'And feel the duvet,' she said. 'This could be filled with feathers too. And mine feels the same, otherwise we could have swopped.'

'Oh no,' groaned Cassie. 'We've got to spend tonight here as well. And I can't sleep without a pillow or quilt.'

'Oh, don't worry about that,' said Becky. 'I'll go and tell Madame.'

When Becky returned a few minutes later with Madame, arrangements had been made to bring some polyester-filled bedding for the two girls. While Madame was talking to Cassie, a maid came in to take away the offending items.

'Would you like to miss the rehearsal this morning, Cassandra?' asked Madame Larette.

'No, it's starting to go off now, Madame, I think I should come.'

'Well, if you're sure. But if you feel too unwell, tell me and you must rest.'

After breakfast, which was as unappetizing as the previous day's meals, the children were driven to the Maison de la Culture, where they would be performing their ballet that evening.

'How are you feeling now, Cassie?' Becky asked her, as they got off the coach in front of the large modern building.

'Still quite breathless,' Cassie admitted. 'I'll have to take it easy in class and save my energy for the rehearsal.'

Madame had already explained to Miss Waters, the young assistant ballet mistress, that Cassie wasn't feeling well.

'Just do the pliés and port de bras, Cassandra,' Miss Waters suggested kindly. 'You can sit out for the rest of the class.'

Although she desperately wanted to join in, Cassie saw the good sense in not over-taxing herself. She took herself off to sit in the auditorium, snug in her track suit, with Teddy Edouard beside her. It wasn't often she had the opportunity to watch the others going through their exercises. Abigail and Poppy with their contrasting colouring – Abigail, black-skinned and dark-haired, Poppy, red-haired and freckle-faced – stood out as the most polished dancers. *It's partly the way they hold themselves*, thought Cassie, *and partly something I can't put my finger on; something which seems to say, I am a dancer.*

Cassie wondered if she had this quality herself when she was dancing. Her eyes flicked to other friends in the class. Becky never really looked comfortable when doing ballet; tap was more her thing. Rhiannon and Celia were technically good but hadn't got that special poise that Abi and Poppy had.

By the time the *Cinderella* rehearsal began, Cassie was feeling much better and could face her solo as the Spring Fairy.

It was to be a full dress rehearsal and the children had been allocated dressing-rooms. Cassie changed into a lemon tutu, sprigged with tiny green leaves and sprinkled with sparkly sequins. In her hair she wore a wreath of artificial spring flowers.

What a contrast she made with Becky, who was now dressed up in her pantomime dame costume for the part of the Ugly Sister. She wore a garish purple dress with a preposterous bustle, red and blue striped socks and a huge mob cap. They looked at their reflections, side by side in the mirror, and laughed.

Miss Oakland, who had taken over from Miss Waters, quickly created a much tenser atmosphere on stage. She stopped the corps de ballet several times in their opening dance.

'No, no, no,' she shouted on one occasion. 'Your arabesques are not in line with one another. Look at your raised arms. They're all different heights. What's the matter with you this morning? Have you forgotten everything I ever taught you?'

Then came the scene when the girls circled the stage, using bouncy steps like pas de basque and temps levée. Miss Oakland clapped her hands together impatiently.

'You look as if you're treading on ice!' she exclaimed. 'Let's put a bit of energy into it!'

'But Miss Oakland,' Celia called out, 'the stage is really slippy, and it slopes too. I'm afraid of falling.'

'Why on earth didn't you tell me before!' Miss Oakland thundered. 'Cassandra!' she commanded, seeing Cassie out of the corner of her eye. 'Go and fetch the resin box immediately.'

Everyone had to put plenty of resin on their shoes before the rehearsal resumed. From then on, the corps de ballet felt more confident and Miss Oakland's criticisms lessened.

When Cassie made her entrance, her spring-like costume helped her to feel her character. Unfortunately, her breathing was still not quite right, which made it very difficult for Cassie to keep up the pace of such a very fast dance. Miss Oakland made the pianist slow the tempo right down.

'We'll do it this way tonight,' she said. 'Better that you get through it, Cassandra, even if it is too slow.'

Cassie felt disappointed. Usually she had so much energy that the fast, crisp pointe work was no problem to her.

She sighed as she left the stage.

'Cheer up!' said Becky. 'It might never happen.'

'My solo's going to look useless at this tempo,' she complained.

30

'Never mind,' said Becky. 'This is only our first night. You'll be better for all the other performances.'

'As long as the pianist doesn't get it into his head to stick at that speed every day!' said Cassie.

'Talk to him about it!' said Becky.

'I will,' said Cassie, picking up her teddy from the backstage area before going back to her dressing-room.

After rehearsal, they were taken back to Belle Vue hotel where they changed into casual clothes and ate a badly-cooked lunch.

'Oh, I can't wait to move on from here,' said Becky. 'I can't stand this food. Where is it we're going next?'

'Rouen,' Cassie answered. 'Are you coming swimming this afternoon? There's an indoor pool at the next complex which we're allowed to use. Everyone seems to be going.'

'Great,' said Becky. 'I haven't had a swim for ages. But are you feeling well enough?'

'Yes, much better. A gentle swim will do me good. I said we'd call for Poppy when we were ready.'

'Do we have to pay to get in?' Becky asked, a little anxiously.

'Yes, but it's not too expensive,' Cassie answered.

'Oh. Would you mind lending me some money?' asked Becky, looking embarrassed.

Cassie was surprised. Normally Becky had far more pocket money than anyone else.

'Have you spent all yours?' she asked.

'No,' said Becky, still looking sheepish. 'The fact is, I've posted all my cash into my magic money-box. It was such fun watching it disappear!'

'Well, you can get it out again!'

'No, that's just the problem – I can't find out how to get it out!'

Cassie burst out laughing. 'Go and fetch it, Becky. Perhaps someone will be able to figure it out at the pool.'

There was a knock on the door. It was Poppy.

'I've just realised I haven't got a swimsuit with me. Either of you got a spare one?'

'Yes, I have,' Becky replied, fishing through one of her cases. 'Here, it's only plain black, but it should fit you.'

'I don't care what colour it is,' said Poppy, 'as long as I can swim in it.'

'I think I'll bring Teddy Edouard,' said Cassie. 'What can he wear for swimming trunks?'

The other two laughed. 'Oh, you are silly, Cassie,' said Poppy.

'Well, he might be lonely if I leave him here.'

'The boys will tease you!'

'I don't care!' Cassie declared.

Half an hour later, the friends found themselves in a very crowded changing-room. Becky had a circle of students around her, trying to find out how to open her money-box, but no one could.

'I think the only thing you can do,' said Poppy, 'is

stick a knife into the slot and tip it upside down.'

Becky groaned. 'That'll take ages!' she complained.

When they tried to go through from the changing-rooms to the pool, an attendant stopped them, shaking his head and pointing to Cassie's teddy.

'Oh poor Edouard. He'll have to sit in the locker instead,' said Cassie. She took him back to the locker section, but he wouldn't fit in with her clothes and shoes, so he had to have a locker to himself.

When she returned, Poppy and Becky were already happily splashing about in the pool. As Cassie sat at the water's edge, paddling her feet, and plucking up courage to jump into the surprisingly cool water, Abigail and Celia emerged from the changing-rooms. Abigail looked lithe and athletic in her electric blue swimsuit, her dark skin making the girls around her look very white. Celia had a towel still wrapped round her and as she got nearer Cassie could hear her arguing with Abigail.

'No, I'm not going in!'

'Don't be silly, Celia,' said Abigail. 'Your swimsuit's fine.'

'I'll look such a fool in it,' Celia cried. 'No one else has got a black school swimsuit on but me.'

Seeing her chance to make amends to Celia for the wrongful accusation, Cassie caught up with them and tapped Celia on the shoulder.

'You're not the only one,' she said. 'Look at Poppy. She's in the pool already. No one's going to look at you, Celia.'

But instead of this making Celia feel better, she turned on Cassie angrily.

'I suppose everyone'll be looking at you, Miss World.'

'I didn't mean it like that at all,' Cassie said helplessly.

Celia drew the towel even more tightly round her and stalked back into the changing-rooms.

'I don't think she'll swim now,' Abigail sighed.

'I don't know how you have so much patience with her!' Cassie cried.

Putting Celia to the back of her mind, she plunged into the pool and enjoyed a refreshing swim with her friends. Some time later, Poppy came up to her and pointed at the clock on the wall.

'It's nearly tea-time already. We'd better get out.'

Cassie looked around. Although still crowded, it was evident that only a few ballet school students were still in the pool. The friends got out and dressed quickly. Celia had waited for Abigail in the changing-room and was still sulking as their little group hurried back to the hotel.

'Oh, I enjoyed that,' said Cassie. 'I feel so much better.'

'Trust you to rub it in,' muttered Celia. 'Well no one was stopping you from swimming,' Cassie retorted.

'Huh,' said Celia. 'I don't know what my mum can have been thinking of, packing my black swimsuit. I've got loads of really nice ones.'

'Don't you pack your own things?' asked Poppy in surprise. She was used to leading a very independent life, living so far away from her home in Australia.

'No, actually, I don't,' snapped Celia. And that was the end of that conversation.

When they got back to the hotel, Celia and Abigail went off to their own room to get ready for tea.

'That's a relief,' said Poppy. 'I don't know how you managed to keep your temper with Celia.'

'Neither do I,' Cassie laughed.

'Will you come with me while I put my swimming things in my room?' asked Poppy.

'OK,' said Cassie. They waited while Poppy hung her wet towel and costume from the window and brushed her hair. Then the three friends went up to the next floor. Becky opened the door of their room. 'Oh, no!' she exclaimed.

'What?' asked Cassie nervously. She and Poppy squeezed in beside Becky in the open doorway. The room was upside down. Costumes, clothes, bedding were all heaped in a jumble on the floor.

'Not again!' cried Cassie.

'And I thought Matthew was sorry for playing that trick on us!' said Becky.

'Do you think it is the boys again?' asked Poppy.

Cassie moved into the room and started picking things up off the floor.

'My bet's on Celia this time.'

'Now, you know you were wrong last time,' Becky warned.

'I know, but she's being really funny with me at the moment.'

'She couldn't have done it, though. She was at the swimming-pool with us,' Poppy pointed out.

'She didn't come in the pool, though. She had plenty of time to run back again!' said Cassie.

'I still think it was the boys,' said Becky.

'Well, whoever it was,' said Cassie, 'I mean to find out!'

'We'd better go down for tea,' urged Poppy.

'You go,' said Cassie. 'Becky and I will straighten this room up. We don't want Miss Oakland seeing it like this. She won't believe someone else did it!'

'OK,' said Poppy. 'I'll try to smuggle something back for you if I can. See you.'

'What a muddle everything's in,' moaned Becky. 'I won't be able to find all my bits and pieces for tonight.'

'It probably didn't take long to make this awful mess,' said Cassie, 'but it certainly takes a while to clear it up again.' A thought struck her. 'There's nothing missing is there, Becky?'

'No, not that I've noticed. My purse is definitely where I left it.'

'Oh drat!' Cassie exclaimed. 'Talking about something missing – I've left Teddy Eduoard behind in the locker!'

'You were daft to take him in the first place!'

'Oh, there won't be time now to go back for him.

36

We'll be going off for our performance in a few minutes!'

Cassie felt quite cross with herself for managing to lose her new teddy so quickly.

4

First Night

Cassie felt exhausted. She longed to climb into bed and fall asleep, but here she was getting her costumes and make-up together for *Cinderella*. She and Becky were the last down to the foyer. Miss Oakland looked up as they walked in and clicked her tongue against her teeth, as she marked off their names on the register.

'The coach is waiting outside,' she announced. 'File out in an orderly manner please!'

They trooped out and boarded the coach. Cassie's stomach began to rumble loudly and Becky giggled.

'I'm starving too!' she said. 'How can we dance on an empty stomach?'

'Never fear, Poppy's here!' said Poppy sitting beside them and offering them each something bundled up in a paper napkin.

'Oh, wonderful!' cried Becky. 'You managed it!'

'It's only a roll and some cheese. They were the only portable things I'm afraid.'

'I don't care what it is,' said Cassie biting into the stale crusty roll. 'I'm famished.'

'Have you asked anyone yet about your room?' Poppy asked.

'Haven't had time,' answered Becky through a mouthful of bread and cheese.

'I'm going to tackle Celia about it before we go on,' said Cassie.

'I don't think you should yet,' Becky cautioned. 'Let's speak to the boys first.'

Cassie reluctantly agreed to Becky's strategy.

Once they had arrived at the Maison de la Culture, Cassie ran off to the dressing-room, where the other girls were already getting changed. Slipping into her lemon tutu and ballet tights, she noticed Celia in the other corner, already applying her make-up. She longed to say something about the messed-up room, but caught Becky's eye. As if she could read her thoughts, Becky frowned at her and shook her head.

When they were both ready, Cassie and Becky went backstage to look for the boys. It wasn't long before they spotted Matthew's ridiculous Ugly Sister costume – an orange flouncy dress with red spots. On his head he wore a tall, white-ringleted wig, which gave him a very comical appearance. For some reason he hadn't worn it at the dress rehearsal.

If Cassie and Becky hadn't been feeling so cross about their room, they would have giggled.

'Bonsoir, ma chere soeur!' he cried, taking Becky by the arm and spinning her round on the spot.

'We are not amused,' said Becky, trying to keep her dignity. 'We've just spent all our tea-time tidying up our room.'

'Well it's your own fault,' said Tom, who had dressed as a courtier. 'You shouldn't leave it in such a mess.'

'*We* didn't leave it in a mess!' said Cassie. 'And we'd like to know who did!'

'Don't look at us!' Matthew said firmly. 'Definitely not guilty.'

'I don't believe you,' said Becky. 'You've been up to tricks ever since we left Dover.'

'Tell them, Tom!' cried Matthew.

'It really wasn't us,' Tom assured them. 'We haven't been near your room since . . . since the last time.'

'Well if anything else happens in our room that's at all suspicious, we're going straight to Miss Oakland,' said Cassie.

'Oh Cassie!' moaned Matthew. 'Please believe us!'

But Cassie and Becky walked off, leaving the boys to stew in their own juice. They returned to their dressing-room, where very soon the call came for beginners, which included Abigail and Becky.

'Oh, I'm not ready for this!' cried Abigail. 'Look, my legs are trembling.'

'You'll be great, Abi,' said Cassie. 'Just don't worry.'

Abigail was normally the most confident of the girl students. It was unnerving to see her like this.

'Come on, Abi,' Becky cajoled her, 'just pretend it's still the dress rehearsal.'

As she was dancing a little later in Act One, Cassie was allowed to watch the beginning of the ballet from the wings along with Poppy.

Abigail, as Cinderella, sat alone on the stage next to the hearth on the painted back-cloth. The curtains were still closed.

As the pianist played the overture, a hush fell over the auditorium. Abigail looked towards the wings for a moment and Cassie gave her the thumbs-up sign, to wish her luck. She knew Abigail was terribly nervous.

'Do you think she'll be all right?' Becky whispered in her ear.

Cassie nodded and put her finger to her lips. The curtains swished apart and the ballet began. A few moments later Becky and Matthew bustled on to the stage, beginning the foolery of the Ugly Sisters, making preparations for the ball. Children in the audience warmed to these two characters immediately. Cassie could hear several of them laughing loudly at their buffoonery.

And then it was Poppy's turn to go on, her lovely costume hidden by a huge black cloak and her face shadowed by its hood. Pretending to be a beggar-woman, she held out her hands at the door of the house. Whereas her two step-sisters had no time for the old woman, Cinderella kindly gave her bread.

As Poppy exited, the students who played the hairdresser, the jeweller and the dancing master moved onto the stage. Becky and Matthew's absurd efforts at learning the graceful court dances provoked more laughter from the audience. Becky came off stage, grinning.

Cassie patted her on the back. 'Well done!' she whispered.

Now came Cinderella's fast solo. She imagined the broom in her hands to be a partner at the Prince's ball and whirled round with it in a pretty dance. Cassie watched Abigail intently. She was definitely not as relaxed as usual and much of the fluidity of the dance was lost.

Very soon it was the turn of the four fairies to appear. They lined up with Cassie in front and limbered up nervously. Jane was Summer, the dark-haired Welsh girl, Rhiannon was Autumn and the Japanese girl, Yoko, danced Winter. Poppy preceded them, revealing her true identity as the Fairy Godmother in her dazzling white dress. She waved her magic wand and her four attendants entered together. Each had a gift which they gave to

Cinderella, before dancing their solos. Cassie, who as the Spring Fairy, went first, brought her a lovely white gown.

She walked forward purposefully to centre-stage, her heart beating hard in her chest. All her tiredness left her as she began to dance. But the pianist had been instructed to keep the tempo slow, and she felt hampered and restrained by this all the way through. Her breathing was no longer a problem and she felt sure she could have tackled it at the normal speed. When a ripple of applause greeted the end of her effort, she felt quite drained and disappointed at her lack-lustre performance.

Of the other soloists, Rhiannon shone, giving a graceful rendering of the Autumn Fairy's dance. She was rewarded with a burst of applause. Her rust velvet and red net tutu set off her dark hair beautifully.

Very soon, Cinderella's ragged appearance had been transformed. She wore a beautiful white gown, a long flowing gold cloak, a tiara for her hair, glistening jewels, and glass slippers. Cassie thought to herself how stunning Abigail looked. In large scale productions, the next scene would have had the Fairy Godmother magically transforming a pumpkin and four mice into a magnificent coach drawn by four horses. But on a small touring production, this had to be missed out. The Act ended with the mimed warning from the Fairy Godmother to come home before midnight.

In Act Two, Cinderella goes to the Ball and dances with the Prince. Cassie and the other fairies weren't needed, so they went back to the dressing-room and played cards to pass the time.

'It's a shame we're not allowed to watch this act,' said Rhiannon, the little Welsh girl.

'Yes,' agreed Cassie. 'I love the funny dances the Ugly Sisters have with their partners.'

The tallest and smallest boys in the second year had been chosen as the partners. Becky and Matthew looked quite comical dancing with them.

'And I love Abi and Ojo's pas de deux,' said Rhiannon. 'It's so flowing and the Prokofiev music is just so beautiful!'

Cassie pictured the dance Rhiannon had mentioned in her mind. It was indeed lovely. How she would have enjoyed dancing it! But she had to admit, even to herself, that Ojo and Abigail made a striking couple, and that, when Abigail wasn't nervous, she made a fabulous Cinderella.

Her thoughts were broken by Becky, Abigail and Celia coming in. They had just finished the Ball scene. It was now the interval, and drinks were sent round to the dressing-rooms.

'Just watch what you're doing with that,' Celia called out, as Cassie picked up her carton, 'or somebody will have a spoiled costume!'

'Oh, haven't you got over that yet?' Cassie cried.

Abigail, tactfully changing the subject, asked everybody how they thought the show was going.

'Everybody looks a bit nervous, I think,' said Cassie, 'but the audience seems to be enjoying it!'

'Abi doesn't look nervous,' scoffed Celia. 'She's dancing wonderfully – a real star. Puts the rest of you right in the shade.'

Abigail looked embarrassed and for the hundredth time Cassie wondered privately how she could stand being friends with Celia.

Then came the call for the beginning of Act Three. Becky had been busy changing in the interval, out of her ball finery into another preposterous dress. She wasn't quite ready, so Cassie, who didn't have a change, helped her put the finishing touches to her outfit.

'How was the last act?' asked Cassie.

'Pretty good, I think,' said Becky. 'The kids in the audience loved that bit when I try to balance on one foot and fall over.'

'I bet!' said Cassie. 'Come on, Becky, hurry up – they're calling for you!'

Becky rushed out, following Abigail back onto the stage. Abigail of course had already been transformed at the end of Act Two, back into her rags.

Cassie watched from the wings, as the two Ugly Sisters got up to their antics once more. It was becoming apparent that Matthew and Becky were the most popular dancers in the show. When they did their tap-dancing duet, there were shouts of 'Encore, encore!' By contrast, Abigail seemed quite under-

46

confident in her dancing. She really didn't look herself.

About halfway through the last Act, when the Prince had identified Cinderella by the glass slipper test, the Fairy Godmother and her four attendants had to reappear. Abigail had a very nifty costume change at this point, back into her lovely ball-gown.

Cassie looked forward to her own second appearance. The pianist seemed to have forgotten the restriction on speed. But just as she was beginning to get into the dance, one of her knees seemed to give way and she stumbled, putting her hand down on the stage to keep her balance. *It must be tiredness* she thought, feeling terribly flustered. She went through the motions of the rest of the dance, but her heart wasn't in it. Her slip just kept flashing through her mind. If she hadn't known the dance so well, she would have certainly started making mistakes. Cassie sank into the final position, as one of the group of four with great relief.

The corps de ballet returned, as Stars and, as Celia performed her short solo, Cassie reflected how lucky she had been to take on the more important role of Fairy Spring, even though she had made a bit of a mess of it.

While Cinderella and her Prince went off to a magical new world which awaited them, the fairies waved goodbye and the curtains closed.

The applause was loud, but fairly brief. After Abigail had been presented with a little posy of anemones, and they'd all curtseyed or bowed, the students went back to their dressing-rooms.

Cassie found herself walking next to Abigail.

'I'm relieved that's over!' exclaimed Abigail.

'So am I! But you'll feel so much better next time,' Cassie promised.

'You were right about me being nervous,' said Abigail. 'I'd much rather hear the truth, than all the over-the-top praise Celia gives me.'

Cassie smiled. 'I'm not feeling too great about my own performance tonight. Things can only get better!'

Becky skipped up behind them. 'You know what it was, Cassie,' she said grinning cheekily. 'You forgot to bring your mascot with you.'

'Teddy Edouard! Oh don't remind me. I must nip across first thing in the morning to see if he's still in the locker.'

The three girls were first back to the dressing-room. Abigail threw herself into a chair.

'I can't wait to get into bed!' she cried.

'You're not the only one!' said Cassie yawning.

'Hey, my case is all messed up!' shouted Becky.

Cassie shot over to look at her own. 'Mine too!' she cried.

As all the other girls came in, it became obvious that all their cases and bags had been rifled through.

'Do you think we've had burglars?' asked Poppy. But when everything had been accounted for, it was plain that nothing had been stolen.

48

'You don't think its those boys again, do you?' said Becky, sighing. 'If it is, it's getting beyond a joke.'

'They were both on stage for the last Act, so how could they have found time?' said Cassie. Tom had been the Prince's Page in this scene and of course both the Ugly Sisters had been on stage nearly to the end.

'Matthew would have had a few minutes at the end,' Becky pointed out. 'He didn't stay in the wings, like I did.'

Cassie had to keep her own suspicions to herself. Celia had been on stage at the very end, that was true. And why should she want to rifle through her own bags? But Matthew and Tom had seemed so definite that they hadn't messed up their hotel room. And surely whoever had done that must also be guilty now?

Her mind raced. Celia hadn't appeared till the finale. She'd had all the rest of the time on her own in the dressing-room. And what better way to cover up than to tamper with her own bag along with the rest?

Cassie glanced over to Celia's corner. She was gabbling away to Abigail, as usual, and at the same time, tidying up her belongings. She didn't look particularly perturbed by the incident.

'Well thank goodness nothing's been taken!' Poppy exclaimed. 'Do you think we'd better report it to Madame?'

'Yes,' said Cassie, watching Celia's face. 'I think we

should. It's happening a bit too often for my liking.'

'Is that really a good idea?' broke in Celia. 'I mean, we might worry her unduly. Nothing's been stolen, has it?'

Cassie looked at her suspiciously. 'Were you in here when the rest of us were on stage after the interval?' she asked.

'Yes,' said Celia, feeling the eyes of the other girls all on her, 'but only for a short while. I went off to find the other Stars and stood in the wings with them for ages.

Celia started to get huffy. 'Anyway, who do you think you are, asking me questions like that?'

'I just wanted to find out how long the dressing-room was empty,' Cassie replied, trying to keep her voice steady.

'You know, I think Celia's got a point,' said Abigail, again trying to prevent a row developing, 'I mean, about telling Madame. While there's a possibility it's one of the students, I don't think we should. Better to deal with it ourselves. Otherwise it could get nasty – people being suspended, that sort of thing.'

'They shouldn't be allowed to get away with it though,' said Poppy.

'I agree with Abi,' said Becky. 'When we've found out who it is, we can take action.'

So Poppy and Cassie were out-voted and the incident was not reported to Madame. Back at the hotel, over a last drink and biscuit, Cassie told her friends of her suspicions about Celia.

'Do you think she'd really be that spiteful?' said Becky.

'I do,' said Cassie. 'Did you notice how eager she was to keep it from Madame's ears?'

'You may be reading too much into that,' said Becky.

'Perhaps you're right,' said Cassie. 'Things will probably look different in the morning.'

'Can't say I'm sorry to be leaving this dump,' said Becky, turning her nose up at her bitter-tasting hot chocolate.

'No,' agreed Cassie. 'Perhaps we're all in for better luck in Rouen!'

~

5

The Booby Trap

'Penny for them!' said Becky the next morning as she caught Cassie day-dreaming.

'Oh,' said Cassie with a start, sitting on her bed, half-dressed. 'I was wondering about our mystery intruder.'

'Perhaps we'll never find out who it is,' said Becky, brushing her hair.

'There must be a way of stopping the culprit,' said Cassie. 'And I still think Celia's the most likely person.'

She got off her bed and began to dress in her practice clothes, topped with the regulation red track suit.

'I shouldn't go accusing Celia,' said Becky. 'You could cause more trouble by doing that.'

'No,' agreed Cassie, 'I won't. But I'm not going to sit back and let my things be messed up again.'

'Well maybe that's the end of it now anyway,' said Becky. 'Ready to come down for breakfast?'

The girls were to have an early breakfast, as the coach which was taking them to Rouen would be there within the hour. They were being driven straight to the venue for their next performance for a rehearsal, before being taken to their new hotel.

Just then, there was a knock at the door. 'It's probably Poppy,' said Becky, and then, more loudly, 'Come in!'

One of the maids entered, carrying a large box of chocolates.

'Bonjour,' they chorused, eyeing the chocolate with great interest.

'Pour Rebecca 'Astings,' she said, looking from one to the other.

'That's me,' cried Becky, grinning. 'I mean, *moi*!'

The maid smiled and handed over the sumptuous-looking box. 'Bon appétit!' she said as she left.

'Fantastic!' said Becky. 'I wonder who—'

'Wait a minute, there's a card with it,' Cassie pointed out. She opened it and inside was a message written in French. The girls tried to make sense of it.

'*Chere Soeur Laide* – that means Dear Ugly Sister, doesn't it?'

54

'Yes,' said Becky. 'I can understand that but the only other words in the letter I can made sense of are *mes enfants*.'

'My children,' mused Cassie. 'And do you recognise the signature? R. Dubonnet?'

'No, never heard of him.'

'Her,' Cassie corrected. 'She's put Madame in brackets after her name.'

Becky looked at the chocolates again and grinned. 'Two each before breakfast?' she suggested.

'Not for me,' said Cassie. 'Not before a coach ride – it might make me sick.'

'That's a point,' said Becky, looking crestfallen.

'We can enjoy them in our new hotel!' cried Cassie. 'Hey, we'd better get down to breakfast. I've also got to go across to the swimming-pool for Teddy Edouard before the coach arrives.'

'I'll find Madame in the dining-room and ask her to translate this card for me,' said Becky.

'Good idea,' said Cassie, 'and I'll ask her how to ask for my teddy back.'

'I still haven't got my money out of that dratted money-box,' said Becky. 'I'd better bring it down with me and try the knife method.'

After breakfast Becky and Poppy decided to accompany Cassie on her errand, but left the French to her! She didn't have to say very much, but even so, she felt quite pleased that she had made herself understood and got her teddy back.

'His ears are a bit crumpled!' she complained, as

they walked briskly back to Belle Vue.

'Well, wouldn't yours be if you'd spent the night in a swimming-pool locker?' laughed Poppy.

'At least our mascot will be coming with us to the theatre tonight. And I've got a feeling he's going to bring us all better luck!'

'My luck's been wonderful already!' Becky exclaimed. 'Wasn't that French lady kind to send Matthew and me a box of chocolates each, just because her children thought we were funny!'

'Yes, lucky you!' said Cassie.

'Don't worry, I'll share them,' Becky said.

Most of the children slept during the coach journey, as the first two days of the tour had proved exhausting. Cassie nudged Becky awake as they approached the centre of Rouen.

'Look, Becky!' she said. 'What an amazing cathedral!'

They gazed out of their windows at the twin-towered building, with its richly-carved facade.

'This is Notre Dame,' exclaimed Madame from behind them. 'The tower on the left is called the Butter Tower.'

'That's a funny name,' said Becky.

'There's a funny story about it,' Madame replied. 'The rich people of the city paid for it for the privilege of eating butter in Lent!'

The coach driver took them straight to the Theatre des Arts, where they disembarked, leaving their main luggage on the coach.

The modern building was used mainly as a music academy, but the children and staff of Redwood Ballet School were pleased to find that its stage was bigger and less slippery than the last one they had just danced on.

Ballet class, taken by Madame, was followed by a rehearsal of some of the weak points which had emerged during last night's performance. In particular, Madame tried to build up Abigail's confidence, and suggested some deep-breathing exercises she could do just prior to going on stage. Soon Abigail was dancing much more freely and expressively, with much of her old sparkle.

Then Madame turned to Cassie and asked if she had had any more breathing problems.

'No, I'm fine now, Madame,' she answered, bobbing a curtsey.

'Très bien,' said Madame. 'I shall be expecting a wonderful solo then from you tonight. Would you like to run through it now?'

'Oh, yes please,' said Cassie.

Once the tempo of the accompaniment was sorted out, Cassie felt on top of the world, doing the fast complicated dance without any problems.

'Bravo!' called Madame, clapping her hands together at the end of Cassie's solo. 'Now don't forget, dance it like that tonight!'

As the girls sat back in the coach once more on the next leg of their journey, Cassie felt a glow of pleasure at Madame's praise. *If only I can pull it off tonight!* she thought to herself.

Their new hotel was much superior to Belle Vue. It was down a wide attractive avenue and inside was much more comfortably furnished. What was even better, the food was delicious. The children made up for two days of poor meals by gorging themselves at lunch-time.

They were given an hour following lunch to unpack and rest. Cassie was sharing a room with Becky, Poppy and Jane this time. For once, they didn't need persuading to lie down.

'Ohh,' groaned Cassie, sinking on to her bed. 'I'm so full, I'll never be able to dance tonight.'

'It'll have gone down by then!' said Becky, laughing. 'You've got to find room for another meal at tea-time first.'

'Don't talk about *more* food!' cried Cassie. 'I wonder if we will be able to stay in our rooms instead of going sightseeing.'

'I doubt it,' said Poppy. 'Madame wants us to see as much of the places we visit as possible.'

'Yes,' Jane ventured timidly, 'she said we'd all got to meet in the dining-room again to sort out groups.'

When the time came, Cassie and Becky were put in Mr Whistler's group, along with Matthew and Tom. Becky still had some suspicions about the boys and hardly acknowledged their greeting, but Cassie was friendly to them. The group began looking around Rouen, and the girls found a variety of shops and buildings to engage their interest.

Mr Whistler took them to see a modern church and monument to the memory of Joan of Arc.

'We're now standing in the Place du Vieux Marche,' announced Mr Whistler. 'It is the ancient market place where Joan of Arc was burned at the stake.'

Cassie shuddered. 'Horrible,' she muttered to Becky.

'Look at the windows in the church,' he directed. 'Aren't they lovely?'

'They don't look modern, like the building,' said Becky, gazing at the wonderful stained glass.

'No, you're right,' said Mr Whistler. 'They're from a sixteenth century church which was bombed in the last war.'

Becky went pink while her favourite teacher was talking to her, and then turned to Cassie in embarrassment.

'I wish I didn't blush so easily,' she whispered.

'It doesn't show half as much as you think it does,' said Cassie, as they followed Mr Whistler to the next site of interest.

They walked down a lively street, called Rue du Gros-Horloge which, as its name suggested, was bridged by a very old clock house with a gigantic, ornate clock.

'Well, you'd have no excuse for being late in this street!' joked Matthew, coming up behind the girls.

'Oh get lost, Matthew,' said Becky.

'What have I done?' cried Matthew.

'It's all right,' said Cassie. 'She still thinks it's you who's messing up our things all the time.'

'Why, has it happened again?' asked Matthew.

'Yes, last night in the dressing-room.'

'How strange,' said Matthew. 'Well, as I said before, not guilty!'

'I believe you,' said Cassie.

Mr Whistler led them to some timber-frame buildings surrounding a flower-filled courtyard.

'This is Aître St-Maclou,' announced Mr Whistler. 'Have a good look at the timbers.'

When the girls got closer, they could see hundreds of stone carvings in the wood.

'They're all horrible things!' cried Cassie in surprise. 'Skulls and bones and coffins!'

'Look over here,' said Becky. 'These look like spades and picks – I don't see the connection.'

Mr Whistler, who had overheard their conversation, came up with the explanation.

'They're grave-diggers' implements,' he explained. 'This used to be a cemetery for plague victims, long ago.'

Many of the students were settling down on the benches provided in the pretty courtyard, and Mr Whistler went over to tell them about the cemetery.

'It's creepy, isn't it?' said Cassie, when he'd gone, 'but fascinating too. Shall we move round the other side to have a look at the rest of the carvings?'

As they rounded the corner, Cassie saw two men ahead, with their backs turned. One wore a navy beret and a navy and white striped jumper. Cassie gasped and drew Becky back into a little recess with her.

'What?' began Becky, but Cassie put her finger to her lips and whispered in her ear.

'I think it's the two men from the gift shop in Amiens!'

Becky, looking a little disbelieving, popped her head out from their hiding-place to have a better look.

'I'm not sure,' she murmured. 'They're too far away. It's probably just the beret and striped jumper. I've seen other men dressed like that.'

Cassie peeped out again, her heart pounding. The men were standing at the corner and seemed to be peering out at the courtyard. From where they were positioned they wouldn't be noticed by anyone inside the courtyard.

'It's like they're spying on Mr Whistler and the others,' whispered Cassie.

'Why would they want to do that?' Becky whispered back.

'I've no idea,' said Cassie. 'I wish they'd turn round. Then we could see if one of them has a scar.'

Cassie peered out from the recess, then ducked back in. 'They're coming this way!' she hissed.

'We can get a close look at them as they go past,' whispered Becky.

'No,' said Cassie. 'I don't want them to get that close! We'd better make a run for it!'

The two girls sprinted off away from the men and back into the courtyard to the comparative safety of the group.

They collided with Matthew and Tom, who were just moving away from the benches.

'What's the hurry?' asked Tom.

'You look as if Dracula's after you!' Matthew exclaimed.

Cassie glanced over her shoulder but the two men had disappeared.

'No time to explain,' she gasped, tugging Becky along with her to join Mr Whistler.

'Everything all right girls?' he asked her.

'Oh, yes thank you, Mr Whistler,' said Cassie, conscious that her story would sound rather silly to a teacher.

Later, when the girls were having a wash in preparation for tea, Becky asked Cassie if she felt sure it was the men from Amiens.

'I mean, you couldn't see the scar, could you?'

'I think I'm sure,' said Cassie and then laughed at the contradiction.

'We didn't get close enough to them,' Becky reminded her. 'Perhaps you've got them stuck in the back of your mind, sort of thing. It could have been anyone really.'

'So, you think it's all in my imagination?' Cassie asked, feeling a little cross. 'Well, OK I'll try to forget about them. But I haven't forgotten about Celia. I've thought up a plan which will stop her little tricks.'

Becky groaned, but had to wait until after tea to find out what Cassie's latest brain-child was.

'A booby-trap!' Cassie announced, when she had got the other girls together in their room. 'Just the thing for protecting us against any more pranks.'

'It's a good idea, I think,' said Poppy, a little dubiously. 'But won't it make a mess?'

'Only if Celia tries anything else,' Cassie replied.

This sounded reassuring, but Becky knew from past experience that Cassie's plans often got them all into trouble.

'We could keep watch instead,' Becky offered.

'Not if we're at the theatre, dancing *Cinderella*,' Cassie scoffed.

Within five minutes, Cassie had her friends scouring the hostel for a bucket, a piece of wood and a rope, while she designed the booby-trap on paper.

When they returned with the objects she'd asked for, she was ready to put her plan into action. Soon, a booby-trap had been rigged up which would cause an unwary intruder to have a bucketful of cold water tipped over his or her head from above the door.

'Perfect,' said Cassie, standing back to admire her design. 'As long as we all remember to take the right precautions when we come in, nothing can go wrong.'

6

A Stitch in Time

'Oh I hope the performance tonight goes better than the last one,' Cassie said to Becky as they sat side by side in the coach.

'It should do,' Becky answered. 'Especially if Abi is more confident. She'll set the tone for everyone else.'

Becky had borrowed a knife from the dining-room and was still fishing round in her money-box with it for the remaining notes and coins.

'Well, I've got enough out for a couple of chocolate bars at least,' she said.

'It's slow progress, isn't it?' remarked Cassie.

Once the ballet was under way, Cassie could see

that Abigail had got over her first night nerves, and was interpreting the role of Cinderella very convincingly. Becky and Matthew were more exuberant and comical than ever, and brought forth roars of laughter when they tried in vain to learn the courtly dances.

'The audience certainly like the Ugly Sisters,' Cassie whispered to Poppy in the wings. 'Wish me luck. I'm on next.'

Poppy drew the black hood over her head and bent over, ready to hobble on to stage like an old beggar woman.

'This gives me back ache,' she moaned just before shuffling out of the wings.

Cassie laughed to herself. If the audience only knew the sort of things that went on backstage! She did some pliés and grandes battements en cloche, to loosen up ready for her own first entrance. One of her ballet shoe ribbons was loose and she stooped to re-tie it. As she did so, there was a snapping noise and she was horrified to find one of her shoulder straps had broken.

She ran towards the dressing-rooms, bumping into Rhiannon on the way.

'You're going the wrong way, Cassie,' said Rhiannon.

'My strap's broken!' gasped Cassie as she rushed off.

'Miss Waters is in dressing-room ten!' Rhiannon called after her.

This useful bit of information saved Cassie a lot of time in hunting round for the teacher, who had the emergency sewing kit with her.

Cassie was in such a dither, she could hardly get the words out when she found Miss Waters, but the teacher quickly spotted what was wrong and got to work with needle and thread immediately.

'It's white cotton,' she explained, 'but there's no time to thread yellow. It won't show on stage anyway. There we are! You'd better hurry!'

Cassie didn't need telling. She sprinted back down the corridor, into the wings and was just in time to see the other three fairies leading on without her. She fell in behind, out of breath, and hoped it wouldn't look too strange when she stepped forward first with Cinderella's gift. *Cinderella's gift! Oh no!* She'd left the ball gown in the wings with Teddy Edouard, when she'd raced off for the repair!

There was nothing for it but to disappear again and fetch it. Luckily the pianist saw she wasn't ready and repeated the last few bars to give her time to come back on stage with the lovely white gown draped over her arms. As she offered the gift to Abigail, she hoped the audience wouldn't be able to see her burning red cheeks.

She took a deep breath and tried to collect herself. Her solo came next and in the state she was in, anything could happen. As she took up her starting pose, centre-stage, she forgot the dark blur of faces in front of her and conjured up an image of how the

Spring Fairy should appear. Although she was still aware of her friends around her on the stage, she was somehow lifted to another level of feeling, where the only important thing was the character she was dancing.

The music and her body seemed to blend into one and for once, the intricate footwork seemed effortless. At the end, she felt as if she had floated through the dance and wasn't the least bit tired. She only came out of her trance-like state when loud applause burst on her ears. Was this for her? She looked forward at the audience in a daze, curtseying mechanically, and only then realising how much they had appreciated her dancing.

A flame of pleasure sprang through her and she stepped, as if on air, to the back of the stage, while Jane walked forward for her solo as Summer.

In the Last Act, the fairies were again very well received, but it was Becky and Matthew's tap duet which nearly brought the house down.

At the final curtain, there were lovely bouquets not only for Abigail and Poppy, but also for the four fairies and the two Ugly Sisters. Matthew grimaced as he received his, but stayed in character, doing a clumsy curtsey with a wild flourish of the hands.

As they spilled offstage, the first thing Cassie heard was Matthew moaning.

'What did they want to give me flowers for?' he wailed. 'Another box of chocolates would have been far better!'

Cassie and Becky laughed at his woeful expression. 'They'll cheer your room up nicely,' said Cassie, clutching her bouquet with pride.

'Yes, but I can't eat them, can I?' he muttered.

'You're getting too fat anyway,' joked Cassie, patting his well-padded bustle.

'Get off,' said Matthew. 'Got any of your chocolates left, Becky?' he asked, hopefully.

'No fear,' Becky answered.

Madame Larette and Mr Whistler were approaching them.

'Marvellous!' breathed Madame. 'Well done, all of you!'

It was bringing my mascot along that did it,' said Cassie, picking up her teddy from his position in the wings.

Madame chuckled. Mr Whistler put an arm round Becky and Matthew.

'And the two Ugly Sisters were hilarious,' he said. He felt especially pleased that the tap dance he had choreographed for them had gone down so well.

Madame smiled at him. 'Are you glad you came on tour with us?' she asked.

'Wouldn't have missed it for the world!' said Mr Whistler. 'I must say these French audiences have been most appreciative.'

Madame and Mr Whistler walked off, deep in conversation, leaving the students to wander back to their dressing-rooms to change.

Cassie still felt very excited from the performance

and, while applying her make-up remover, couldn't stop talking to Becky.

'I can see we'll be kept awake half the night!' Poppy remarked to Jane.

'I feel as if I could fall asleep on my feet,' said Jane.

By the time every trace of make-up had been removed, and all the costumes had been re-packed, Cassie had started to yawn too. All the excitement had drained from her. A tired, flat feeling was what was left in its place.

They all climbed wearily into the coach.

'You're a cheerful lot!' muttered Frank, the coach driver, sarcastically. It was the first time Cassie had known him speak to any of the students. Whenever he talked to Madame or Miss Oakland, he sounded grumpy.

Travelling back to the hotel, the dancers struggled to keep their eyes open. They dragged themselves up the stairs and slowly made their way along their corridor.

'Oh! I've just remembered!' cried Cassie suddenly. 'The booby-trap!'

'I'd forgotten,' Becky admitted. 'Wouldn't it have been awful if we'd gone barging in without undoing the rope first?'

Cassie didn't answer. She had reached the door to their room slightly ahead of the others and had stopped in front of it.

'What's the matter?' asked Poppy from behind Becky.

'Shh,' warned Cassie. 'The door's ajar.'

She put her hand through the gap and felt for the rope.

'It's been disconnected!' she whispered back at her three friends.

'Did anyone else know about it?' asked Jane.

The others shook their heads.

'I can't hear anyone in the room,' said Cassie. 'Let's go in.'

They all charged in together, just in case. But the room was empty. And very wet. The trap had been set off.

Becky groaned, while Poppy and Jane looked about them in dismay. The bucketful of water had not only drenched the carpet, but had also soaked two of their beds.

Cassie was by now wide awake and glowing with excitement.

'It worked, it worked!' she sang, doing a little skip. 'Celia must have got soaked!'

'But Cassie!' cried Becky, exasperated by all the mess. 'We're going to get absolutely done for this!'

'It's only water!' said Cassie airily. 'It'll dry.'

'It couldn't have been Celia,' Poppy broke in. 'She didn't have the opportunity tonight.'

Cassie plonked herself down on her bed, which was dry fortunately, and scratched her head. 'Oh dear, you're right.'

'Well, who on earth has been into our room?' asked Becky.

'I think I can guess what's happened,' said Poppy slowly. 'A maid or cleaner or someone has come in and triggered the booby-trap.'

'Oh no!' cried Cassie. 'They're bound to complain about us to the manager.'

'I knew this would get us into trouble,' said Becky.

'Oh, what can we do?' asked Jane nervously.

'I don't know where to start,' said Becky, looking around the room helplessly.

'Why don't you get rid of the bucket and rope and I'll see if I can find a mop,' Cassie suggested.

'And I'll strip this wet bedding off,' volunteered Poppy. 'Where are Jane and I going to sleep tonight?'

'You can share with me, and Jane with Becky,' said Cassie. 'And we'll drape the bedding out of the window tomorrow morning. It'll soon dry in the breeze.'

As Becky opened the door, holding the bucket and rope, she almost fell over Celia.

'Hi, you guys!' said Celia. Her expression changed as she took in the state of the room. A look of pleasure passed over her face.

'What have you been up to?' she asked.

'Oh, nothing much,' said Cassie quickly. 'Bit of an accident with a glass of water, that's all.'

'A bucket-sized glass, I should think,' said Celia. 'Uggh! The carpet's soaking. My socks are all wet now!'

'Serves you right for coming in uninvited,' said Poppy sharply. Celia was the last person they wanted

72

nosing about just at that moment.

'Mmmm,' said Celia thoughtfully. Cassie could see her putting two and two together. 'Well, I better go and get into some dry socks. See you later, guys!'

As she padded off down the corridor, Cassie sighed. 'Well, if the cleaner hasn't given us away, Celia soon will. You'd better go and find a mop, Becky. And we'll do our best with our bath towels.'

Five minutes later there was an official-sounding knock on the door.

'Come in!' they called.

Miss Oakland walked in, frowning. 'This is disgraceful!' she exclaimed. 'However did it happen?'

Cassie thought it best to tell her the truth. 'We . . . we made a booby-trap, Miss Oakland. But one of the cleaners must have come in while we were doing the show and . . .'

'But why?' Miss Oakland interrupted.

'Well, our things have been tampered with a couple of times and we wanted to put a stop to it.'

'Say no more!' thundered Miss Oakland. 'I don't have to ask whose ridiculous idea this was!'

She glared accusingly at a blushing Cassie.

'I thought as much,' said Miss Oakland. 'Have you no sense, girl? People messing with your things, indeed! This sort of behaviour won't do at all – especially in a hotel!'

'I'm sorry, Miss Oakland, I just didn't think . . .'

'No, you're not very fond of thinking, are you, Cassandra?' She sighed and looked at the mess. 'I'll get someone to come up and take away this wet bedding. Are the mattresses wet too?'

'Ours are,' said Jane, indicating herself and Poppy.

'Right, you two get a night bag organized and come to my room. I'll squeeze you in one of the other dormitories.'

She took a last look at the room and tutted. 'I don't know what's got into you all! Have you discovered yet who set the trap off and got a soaking?'

'No,' replied Becky, 'we haven't.'

'Well, *no more* silly ideas, is that quite clear?'

'Yes, Miss Oakland,' said Cassie.

Left alone, Cassie and Becky got ready for bed, making detours round the soggy bit in the middle of the floor.

'So, Miss Oakland hadn't been tipped off by the hotel staff then,' said Becky. 'She asked us if we knew who'd set the trap off.'

'No,' Cassie agreed, 'so that leaves Little Miss Sneak herself.'

'I wonder who did set off the trap?'

'It could still have been a cleaner. One with a sense of humour, or maybe a lazy one, who couldn't be bothered to clear it all up!'

Becky looked doubtful. 'Or a cat even?'

'Cats don't turn doorknobs, Becky!'

Right on cue, their doorknob turned, making them both jump in unison.

Abigail poked her head round the door. 'I just popped round to say bad luck,' she said.

'It wasn't a question of luck,' said Cassie. 'Celia must have told on us.'

'Oh no,' said Abigail. 'She didn't tell me that.'

'Afraid so,' said Becky. 'Miss Oakland was fuming.'

'At least she couldn't put us in detention!' said Cassie.

'Oh, I'm going to stop speaking to Celia,' said Abigail. 'She really shouldn't go telling tales. It's awful.'

Cassie and Becky exchanged glances. This was going to be another down in the up-and-down friendship of Abigail and Celia.

'See you tomorrow, anyway. Have a good night!'

'Thanks,' said Cassie.

'Paris tomorrow!' Abigail exclaimed. 'The Eiffel Tower, the Arc de Triomphe!'

'Oh I'd forgotten!' shrieked Cassie, her eyes opening wide.

'Forgotten Paris?' asked Becky.

'No, my *birthday*,' said Cassie. 'I'm thirteen tomorrow!'

7

Birthday in Paris

Cassie woke early. Her first thought was, *It's my birthday* and her second was, *I wish I were at home!* Birthdays were never quite the same away from her family and today she was actually in a different country! But her pangs of homesickness didn't last very long, because Becky woke up almost immediately and bounced over to her friend's bed with a little parcel and a card.

Always thrilled by presents, Cassie tore apart the wrapping paper feverishly, revealing a little china ballerina in a box.

'Oh, she's lovely,' breathed Cassie, taking out the

figurine for a better look. 'Thank you, Becky!'

'I'm glad you like it,' said Becky, stretching her arms out wide. 'It's going to be a hectic sort of birthday for you. I suppose we'd better get down to some packing.'

'Yes, on the move again,' said Cassie. 'Exciting though, isn't it?'

As if in answer, the door burst open and Poppy rushed into the room, followed more sedately by Jane.

'Happy Birthday!' cried Poppy, giving Cassie a big hug.

The girls had made her a card and Poppy surprised her with a present she'd been hiding behind her back.

'It's not much, I'm afraid,' said Poppy.

But Cassie's eyes lit up when she found it was a box of chocolates. She offered them round and promised her friends more later, once they had reached Paris.

'Yes, we'd better get on with our packing,' said Poppy, glancing at her watch.

As Cassie and Becky went down to the dining-room, they half expected every hotel worker they met to accost them with protests about the booby-trap. But the way down was uneventful and they sat down to a breakfast of croissants and crusty bread, feeling relieved.

Several of her friends came over and wished Cassie a happy birthday, and by the time they were all sitting on the coach, everyone seemed to know about it. To Cassie's surprise, they all sang 'Happy Birthday' to her – staff included!

They settled down for the journey from Rouen to Paris, some with Walkmans, others with books or magazines, but most just content to chatter.

Cassie, Poppy, Becky, Jane and Abigail were sitting along the back seats. As the journey wore on, Cassie began to think about the men they had seen at the plague cemetery. Even though Becky hadn't recognised them, Cassie was pretty sure they were the same two she had seen arguing in the shop in Amiens.

Thinking back to that day in the shop, was it possible that she and Becky had looked rich and had seemed easy targets? She nudged Becky.

'You know that day in Amiens when we bought Teddy Edouard and your money-box?'

'Yes?'

'Well, did you have any of your nice jewellery on?'

Becky thought back. 'I may have worn my gold chain and bracelet.'

'Yes, I think I remember now – you did. I haven't seen you in them since.'

'The day after that I gave them to Madame for safe-keeping. She suggested it actually. What's all this about anyway?'

'Oh, nothing,' said Cassie evasively. Becky would only tell her to stop thinking about the men again.

A nasty thought struck her. Perhaps it had been

the men who had got into their room and set off the booby-trap. And maybe it had even been them the other times, when their belongings had been messed up. A shiver of fear ran down her spine. She couldn't hold it back from Becky any longer.

'Becky, what if it was the men from Amiens who were in our room yesterday?'

'Don't be silly, Cassie. Just because you saw a couple of men who looked a bit like them in the plague cemetery. You're getting carried away.'

Cassie didn't say any more. Perhaps Becky was right and there would be no more unexplained happenings in Paris.

A cheer went up in the coach as the Eiffel Tower came into sight.

'I'm looking forward to this bit of the tour,' said Cassie.

They were to take part in workshops at a leading Parisian ballet school and put on a joint performance on their second night, at the well-known Georges Pompidou Art Centre.

Madame had told them they would have their biggest audience here and one which would probably know a fair amount about ballet.

They arrived at their new hotel on the outskirts of Paris, just in time for a lovely lunch of mushroom soup, garlic bread and cheese.

'Ooh, that was yummy,' said Becky, arranging her cutlery on her empty plate. 'Looks like we're going to be lucky here.'

Their hotel, the Parisienne, however, was not so comfortably furnished as the one in Rouen. Cassie, Becky and Poppy found they were sharing a small, rather dingy attic bedroom, with only a threadbare rug on the varnished floorboards.

Looking at it, Cassie felt another pang of homesickness. She decided to go down to the payphone on the ground floor, and ring her parents. Her money seemed to get eaten up amazingly quickly and she only managed a brief conversation with her mother. As she put the phone down, she was surprised to find that her eyes were smarting with tears. She hurried past groups of students back to the attic bedroom.

'What's the matter?' asked Becky, noticing at once that something was wrong.

'Just a bit of homesickness,' Cassie replied. 'I've always managed to have my birthday at home before. Mum usually makes me one of her scrummy cakes.'

'Never mind,' said Poppy. 'You're doing what you like doing best on your birthday. That's special!'

'You're right,' said Cassie. 'Once I get stuck into the workshop, I'll be fine.'

'It would ruin my birthday,' Becky broke in. 'The thought of two-and-a-half hours ballet classes.'

Cassie smiled. 'There's going to be a character class, don't worry.'

'But no tap!' Becky pulled a face.

The girls got ready, putting on their leotards and tights underneath track suits and plaiting and pinning up each other's hair. When they got down to the foyer to meet everyone else, Cassie realised she'd forgotten something and started back up the stairs.

'Forgotten your ballet shoes?' called Becky.

'No, Teddy Edouard!' cried Cassie. 'Mustn't go without our mascot.'

About an hour later, she was warming up in the studios of the Paris Ballet School, feeling much happier. They had been split up into groups. Cassie's group included Poppy, Abigail, Rhiannon and Celia but not, unfortunately, Becky, who had been placed in a lower group. There was a mixture of French and English girls in each group.

Their first class was taken by Madame Larette. This presented no problems to anyone, as Madame was able to speak English *and* French. Instructions just took a little longer than usual. It was always Madame's way to explain what she wanted very carefully. She had a slow, methodical approach, unlike Miss Oakland's lightning demands, and it soon became obvious that the French girls liked Madame. As they went through the pliés and battements that she had done hundreds of times before, Cassie's spirits lifted. The familiar movements were comforting, because the concentration had to be so firmly placed on the exercises.

Character class which followed was taken by Mlle Jacques, a painfully thin and gaunt-looking French woman. The students learned a Russian-flavoured national dance, in pairs. As ever, there weren't enough boys to go round, so Cassie ended up partnering Poppy.

The dance was lovely, with grand sweeping pas de basques and promenades. Mlle Jacques spoke quite good English but her manner was very sharp. Cassie noticed that some of the French children seemed quite frightened of her.

'Glad we haven't got her at Redwood,' Poppy whispered.

'Me too,' Cassie whispered back. 'Even Miss Oakland seems nice by comparison.'

In the short break which followed, there were quite a few complaints about Mlle Jacques. Cassie could hear Celia's voice above the rest. She sounded quite resentful.

'Are you speaking to Celia yet?' Cassie asked Abigail.

Abigail shook her head. 'I've told her I will when she admits sneaking on you and apologises.'

'I think you'll have to wait a long time for that,' said Cassie.

In the next session, they were taught an extract from one of Juliet's solos from *Romeo and Juliet*. Their new teacher was Mme Fleurette, petite, pretty and quite charming. She didn't attempt to speak any English, so Cassie and her friends had to listen and watch extremely attentively, in order to keep up with the French girls. Although this was a strain, Cassie didn't mind. She was delighted to be learning such a wonderful solo, to Prokofiev's expressive music.

The first sequence of steps they had to master involved rising onto pointe in arabesque. It called for immense strength in the supporting leg and foot. Cassie was concentrating so hard on what she was doing that she didn't at first realise that Mme Fleurette was speaking to her. And even then, she couldn't pick out any of the words except *pieds*. She glanced at her feet. They seemed to be arched and turned out correctly. What was wrong?

But then she saw the teacher smiling and nodding to her and realised she was *complimenting* her on her feet.

The teacher's method seemed to be one of praise and encouragement, rather than one of criticism, which was a welcome change. Most of the girls seemed to thrive in the more relaxed atmosphere. But Celia seemed to see it as an opportunity to play up, muttering under her breath every time Mme Fleurette gave instructions in French.

When the teacher took no notice of her, Celia was encouraged to whisper to Abigail: 'She's working us too hard! I'm exhausted. Who wants to learn Juliet's soppy solo anyway?'

'Do be quiet!' hissed Abigail. 'She's a really nice teacher.'

'She's rubbish, if you ask me,' Celia went on.

A feeling of unease spread through the room. Cassie would have loved to have put a big piece of sticky-tape over Celia's mouth.

Half the class had to run over to one corner, while the other went through the first part of the solo. Cassie found herself standing next to Celia and Abigail in the corner. She could see Abigail was very cross.

'Why on earth can't she speak English?' Celia whispered.

'Oh shut up!' Cassie said, as loudly as she could.

'Yes, shut up, Celia,' Abigail chipped in.

Mme Fleurette stopped the class. In perfect English she asked Celia to step forward. Celia blanched, realising the teacher must have understood everything she'd said.

'You have been disruptive and rude and I would like you to leave my class.'

'I'm sorry, Madame,' Celia stammered and ran out with a very white face.

The rest of the session ran very smoothly and Cassie was sorry when they ran out of time. They hadn't been able to learn the end of the solo. She promised herself that one day, when she was older, she would learn it all and maybe even dance the role on stage.

Cassie had been very impressed by the high standard of the French girls in the group. One in particular seemed outstanding, not only in her technique, but also in her expressiveness. By chance, she stood next to Cassie and Poppy in the changing-room and introduced herself as Claudette. She wanted to know how old they were.

'Twelve,' said Poppy.

'Thirteen – today!' said Cassie.

Claudette looked surprised. 'It is your . . . *anniversaire* . . . today? Mine *aussi*!' she exclaimed.

The three girls giggled and chatted, half in French and half in English, all the way to the dining-hall.

The French ballet school had prepared a very nice buffet tea for their visitors. Cassie and her friends were joined at their table by Becky, who announced she was starving.

'What's new?' said Cassie, laughing. 'Did you enjoy your classes?'

'Character yes, ballet no. Our last teacher was awful, honestly.'

'Who was it?' asked Poppy.

'Mlle Jacques,' said Becky.

'Say no more,' said Cassie. 'We had her for character.'

'You poor things,' groaned Becky. 'We had an absolutely gorgeous man for character.'

'Oh, has Mr Whistler come up against some competition?' Cassie asked mischievously.

Becky blushed. 'Oh no, he couldn't compare with Mr Whistler!'

'Oh look,' said Poppy. 'They're bringing something in!'

The hubbub of voices in the room rose to an excited pitch as the chef carried in an enormous chocolate cake, bearing thirteen small pink candles.

The Directeur of the school stood up and, first in French, then in English, formally welcomed the English visitors and announced it was Claudette's and Cassandra's birthday.

There were cries of '*bon anniversaire*' and '*happy birthday*' from all round the room. A cheer went up as Cassie and Claudette stepped forward to blow out their candles together.

Tears stood in Cassie's eyes, not from homesickness any more, but from happiness. Her birthday had turned out to be a special day after all.

8

No Adults Admitted

The group of English students didn't get back to their hotel until nearly eleven o'clock that night. Cassie, Poppy and Becky tumbled into bed, too tired even to wash.

'My legs are killing me,' Becky groaned.

'It's been a wonderful day though, hasn't it?' said Cassie, yawning. 'I really enjoyed *La Fille Mal Gardée*.'

The French students had put on the ballet for their visitors in the evening.

'Yes, I haven't seen it before,' said Poppy. 'It's so funny, isn't it?'

'And wasn't Claudette brilliant?' exclaimed Cassie.

89

The others agreed. Claudette had danced the role of Lise, the leading female part, with great professionalism.

'But Lise's mother was the best,' argued Becky.

Cassie and Poppy laughed. The part had been played by one of the boy students.

'I loved his clog dance,' said Becky.

'Mmm, I thought you would, somehow!' Cassie answered.

'I am glad we had chance to watch it,' said Poppy. 'Tomorrow night we'll be backstage.'

'I feel a bit nervous about tomorrow night,' said Cassie. 'It's going to be a very big audience.'

The two schools were going to present a joint programme: *La Fille Mal Gardée* in the first half and *Cinderella* in the second.

'Must go to sleep now,' mumbled Becky.

Within minutes they were all asleep.

The next morning was warm and sunny – ideal for sightseeing. But first they had ballet class and rehearsal, back at the studios.

Cassie ran up to Claudette while they were waiting for the ballet mistress to arrive.

'You were brilliant last night ... umm, *merveilleuse*!'

'Thank you,' said Claudette, beaming. 'And you are first dancer in *Cinderella* tonight?'

'No, no,' said Cassie. 'Abi over there is Cinderella. I am Fairy Spring.'

'Oh, I am surprised. You are so good.'

It was Cassie's turn to be pleased. 'Good luck tonight.'

'And for you also,' Claudette replied.

Their joint ballet class was taken by Madame Larette once more. Cassie noticed Celia was missing. During the break for a drink and biscuit, she asked Abigail about it.

'She got a terrible ticking off from Miss Oakland yesterday,' Abigail replied, 'and she's been moved down a group.'

'Are you speaking to her yet?'

'Yes, I have been today,' answered Abigail sheepishly. 'I felt a bit sorry for her.'

'Ah well,' said Cassie, 'I think she's had enough punishment now.'

After break, the English and French students separated for rehearsals of their ballets. There would be no opportunity to rehearse at the Pompidou because there were always so many bookings there. It wasn't ideal, but the children had already adapted to two different-sized stages, so the staff felt they would cope with it.

Miss Oakland supervised the *Cinderella* rehearsal, which ran quite well. Cassie thought by now everyone should know what they were doing inside out and half-wondered why they were having yet another rehearsal. But Miss Oakland was in a critical mood and stopped several of the dances in mid-flow for minor technical faults.

Cassie hoped she wouldn't pick any faults with

her solo. She was afraid that might make her lose her confidence again. Feeling nervous, Cassie began the Spring variation. She found it extremely difficult to focus her mind on what she was doing.

Miss Oakland stopped her quite quickly.

'If you would take your mind off booby-traps and put it on your dancing, it would be a great improvement, Cassandra!' she cried.

Cassie continued, but Miss Oakland interrupted her continually. She was glad when the ordeal was over and she could escape to the wings.

Poor Rhiannon did not fare much better. She got muddled in her Autumn solo and ended up in tears, after a scolding. Then when it was Celia's short Star solo near the end of the ballet, Miss Oakland started criticizing Celia's port de bras.

'Arms are just as important as legs, Celia,' Miss Oakland declared. 'In fact everything in a dancer's body is of equal importance. Use your arms. Use your head and your whole body. We don't want to watch a puppet on a string, do we?'

'No, Miss Oakland,' said Celia. But under her breath, she muttered, 'I'm fed up with people going on at me.'

'What was that, Celia?' asked Miss Oakland, with an edge to her voice.

'Oh nothing, Miss Oakland,' said Celia meekly.

'I won't have you muttering under your breath when I'm talking to you, do you understand?'

'Yes, Miss Oakland. Sorry.'

At last, the rehearsal was over. The girls wandered down to the dining-hall to eat their packed lunches, which had been provided by the hotel. Cassie especially enjoyed her hard-boiled egg. Becky finished first and complained she was still hungry.

'Have you brought some money with you?' asked Cassie.

'Yes.'

'Well, you'll be all right then. There'll be plenty of shops when we look round the city this afternoon.'

As there were so many places of interest in Paris, and limited time, a vote was taken by Madame in the dining-room, with the majority choosing the Eiffel Tower and shopping. After the Tower, Madame was to take them to a big new shopping and entertainment centre called the Forum.

Before they set off, they were split into groups and allocated a tutor. Cassie and her friends were with Miss Oakland, which didn't look promising; she was in a foul mood. They would have to tread very carefully.

They could see the Eiffel Tower throughout their journey to it. Madame explained that it could be seen from all over Paris.

'When it was first built in the 1880s,' she said, 'it was the tallest monument in the whole world!'

Arriving at the foot of it, Cassie was disappointed to see queues at the entrance.

Luckily, the weather had stayed fine and they

passed the time in the queue by watching a Punch and Judy show.

'Oh I love it when the crocodile pinches the sausages,' cried Becky, laughing as much as the small children who were watching.

At last it was their turn to get in the lift and go up the Tower.

'It's *brilliant* up here!' Cassie exclaimed. 'Look, you can see right across Paris. We're so high up.'

'Give me Punch and Judy any day,' said Becky. 'I don't like heights.'

Miss Oakland took her party to the Forum next. It was a pedestrian-only complex which housed a huge variety of shops, several cinemas, a children's theatre, a holograph museum and a waxworks.

The children were allowed to browse around the shops. Cassie bought some small gifts to take back for her family – a miniature Eiffel Tower for her parents and a key-ring with a torch for Adam, but she couldn't quite decide what to get for Rachel, who was too little for most of the gifts.

'What about a cuddly toy?' suggested Poppy.

'That's a good idea,' Cassie agreed.

They soon found a gift shop, which sold soft toys. Becky came across a teddy which looked just like Teddy Edouard.

'I think I'll buy him,' she said. 'It'll be fun having twins, won't it?'

Cassie scrutinized the teddy. 'Not an identical twin. There's something different about his face.'

'Really? I can't see it,' said Becky.

Cassie picked up a pink rabbit and they took the toys to the counter.

'I think I'll call him Pierre,' said Becky.

They walked back to Miss Oakland, who was sitting down on a bench.

'The others are still shopping,' she said. 'You can have another fifteen minutes.'

As they strolled away again, they came across a children's garden just off the square.

'That looks nice,' said Becky. 'Shall we go in?'

They ran back to Miss Oakland to ask permission.

'No, I don't think so, Rebecca. I want all of you in one place so I can keep my eye on you.'

'But it's just over there,' said Cassie. 'If you stand up, you can see it clearly.'

'Well, all right then,' Miss Oakland agreed reluctantly, 'but check your watches and be here by four o'clock, or you'll have me to contend with.'

'Thank you, Miss Oakland,' the three girls chorused, before racing off to the garden.

It was prettily laid out but best of all, there was strictly no admittance to adults!

'Miss Oakland can't come and breathe down our necks in here!' said Becky.

There were swings and climbing apparatus, but the girls felt a bit big to go on anything except the swings.

'This reminds me of being at home,' said Cassie. 'I still often have a go on the swing in my garden.'

As Cassie looked across the flower beds, her heart skipped a beat. Leaning against the other side of the fence, staring in her direction, were two men.

'Becky, look over by the exit!' cried Cassie. 'Isn't it those men from Amiens?'

'Oh not again, Cassie,' Becky moaned. 'You've got them on the brain!'

'But have a good look!'

'Those two have both got beards!' Becky exclaimed. 'Our two were clean-shaven. What *is* the matter with you, Cassie?'

'But I know it's them,' said Cassie. 'I just sort of know it. They're probably wearing false beards.'

'Oh, Cassie, you are funny,' said Poppy, tittering.

'Don't laugh at me,' Cassie snapped. 'Those two are following us for some reason. Believe me!'

'They're not dressed the same,' said Becky.

'Well, if you won't be convinced, we'll casually walk over in their direction and when we're close enough, we'll be able to see if one of them's got a scar or not.'

'Yes, that would settle it,' said Poppy.

Cassie felt a bit apprehensive about getting closer to them, but felt comforted by the railing which separated them and also by the fact that there was an attendant at the entrance who wouldn't allow adults past him.

The three girls pretended to be deep in conversation, not looking towards the men at all until they were reasonably close. When Cassie did look up, the men were still watching them, which was very unnerving. The girls moved away again and compared notes.

Cassie had to admit she couldn't see a scar, because of the huge bushy beards the men were wearing.

'But I'd bet on my life that those beards are false,' she said. 'And their build and eyes were the same.'

'What did you think, Becky?' Poppy asked.

Becky hesitated. 'Well, I thought it was just Cassie's imagination again . . . but now I'm not so sure. There was a look of the men from Amiens. And they *were* watching us.'

'Just like they were watching the other students, when we saw them in Rouen,' said Cassie.

'Oh, you two are giving me the creeps,' said Poppy. 'Come on, it's two minutes past four. We'd better get back pretty sharpish, or we'll get done!'

'Hang on,' said Cassie, restraining Poppy. 'Look where they're standing – right by the exit. We'll have to walk straight past them.'

'See what you mean,' said Becky. 'I don't think it's a very good idea.' She clutched her new teddy to her.

'Oh no,' groaned Poppy. 'It must be catching. You're getting as bad as Cassie.'

'I don't care what you say,' Cassie said, jutting out her chin. 'I'm not walking past those men.'

'Well, I'd rather face the men than Miss Oakland,' said Poppy.

'I know,' said Cassie, 'if we go across behind the

swings, we should be able to climb over the railings. Do you see – there are some bushes in front of them?'

'Right,' said Becky. 'We'll have to be careful the attendant doesn't see us.'

They sauntered over to the swings, trying to look innocent, and then dashed through the bushes and scrambled over the railings. They hared off round the perimeter of the garden and came back to the square where Miss Oakland and the others were waiting. The men hadn't followed them.

'I don't think they saw where we went!' said Becky.

'No, they're probably still watching for us at the exit,' giggled Cassie.

'Shh,' warned Poppy. 'Miss Oakland's glaring at us.'

'I thought I told you girls to be back here no later than four. It is now precisely seven minutes past. I've a good mind to ban you from any future sightseeing.'

The girls apologised, but Miss Oakland remained in a bad temper. She even had a row with Frank, the coach driver, who had been smoking on the coach.

'Two miseries together, if you ask me,' said Becky, as they listened to Frank's surly replies.

'I'll be glad to get back to the hotel,' said Cassie. 'Those men gave me a fright.'

'Why do you think they're following us?' Becky asked.

Cassie considered. 'Perhaps it was something we took from the shop that they didn't want us to have?'

98

'But we only bought your teddy and my money-box!' Becky exclaimed.

'And the postcards,' added Cassie.

'Do you think we should tell Madame?'

'I don't know,' Cassie replied. 'I'd like to tell her, but, well, there's not much hard evidence, is there? She'd probably think it was just my imagination.'

'She wouldn't be the only one,' said Poppy.

'It's a pity we can't set up another booby-trap . . .' Cassie mused.

'Oh no,' said Becky, with feeling. 'I'm not risking getting on the wrong side of Miss Oakland again this holiday.'

'Well,' sighed Cassie, 'we'll just have to keep our eyes and ears open, won't we?'

9

Two Teddies

'Teddy Edouard, meet Teddy Pierre,' said Becky, manipulating the two bears. The girls were in the hotel dining-room, awaiting their tea.

'They've already met upstairs,' said Cassie.

'They haven't been formally introduced,' Becky corrected her.

Madame approached their table. 'I'm asking everyone to have a lie down for half an hour before tonight's performance. Sightseeing can be rather tiring.'

'And alarming,' said Cassie, as Madame moved off to another table.

'Oh, don't remind me,' said Becky.

In their room after tea, the girls tried to rest, but couldn't.

'Where's that money-box?' Cassie asked Becky.

'Here it is,' said Becky, putting it on Cassie's bed.

'Have you emptied it?'

'I think I got all the money out,' Becky replied. 'It took me absolutely ages!'

Cassie shook it. 'Well, there's nothing rattling in it. But it would be quite good for hiding something small inside it, wouldn't it?'

Becky began to guess what was going through Cassie's mind. 'No, you can't take it apart. That would ruin it!'

Cassie shrugged. 'It's your money-box. I'd just like to get to the bottom of why these men are following us.'

'But we don't know for sure what they're after,' said Becky.

'Won't you let me make another booby-trap?' asked Cassie.

'No, definitely not,' said Becky.

'I promise not to get everything wet again,' pleaded Cassie. 'We've got to have some protection, haven't we?'

Becky and Poppy considered. 'I suppose you're right,' Poppy admitted, reluctantly.

'But please don't get us into any more trouble, Cassie,' Becky added.

Cassie's face lit up. 'I'll just nip over and ask

Matthew if we can borrow his book.'

'Which book?'

'You know: *Crazy Practical Jokes*.'

When she returned with it, Cassie spent the remainder of the rest period thumbing through its pages.

'I've hit on just the thing,' she said in the end. 'But I think I'll ask the boys to give us a hand to prepare it.'

'Is that wise?' asked Becky.

Cassie shrugged. 'We need several chairs. If we can borrow some from their rooms and perhaps Jane's and Rhiannon's, we should have enough.'

'We're going to have to work quickly then,' said Poppy. 'We haven't long before the coach arrives to take us to tonight's performance.'

'Come on then,' said Cassie. 'I'll explain as we go along.'

'Have you had a nice rest, girls?' asked Madame, as they came down into the foyer with their costume bags and Teddy Edouard.

The coach was waiting outside and they hurried on to it. Everyone was feeling a little apprehensive about the forthcoming show, mainly because they hadn't had the chance to practise on stage.

As they drew up outside the Pompidou Arts Centre, there were gasps of astonishment. It was a vast, brilliantly-lit, brightly-coloured, ultra-modern building. But what was so unusual was that the stairs, escalators, elevators, vent shafts and gas and water pipes were all on the *outside* of the building!

There were queues for the escalators, and on the piazza in front of the building were crowds of onlookers watching a white-faced mime artist and some jugglers performing in the open air.

'There are so many people!' Cassie exclaimed. 'I hope they're not all coming to watch us!'

The girls were relieved to find that as performers, they didn't have to wait in a queue. They were soon hurrying through a succession of doors to the large dressing-room they'd be sharing with all the other Redwood girls.

Cassie undressed and stepped into her tutu. The zip got caught at the bottom, in the top layer of net.

'Oh Becky, can you see if you can sort this zip out for me?' she asked, as Becky was pulling on her stripy tights.

Becky wrenched the zip to get it free, tearing the top layer of net as she did so.

'Oh, Cassie, I'm sorry!' she cried as they looked at the damage.

'I'd better go and find Miss Waters again!' said Cassie. 'Don't worry. It wasn't your fault.'

Inwardly, Cassie felt sorry that her tutu had been ripped, as it would never be possible to mend the net satisfactorily. Miss Waters did her best with needle and thread, but even she admitted there wasn't a lot she could do to disguise it.

'At least it's at the back, Cassandra, and of course details don't really show up much on stage.'

'Thanks, Miss Waters,' said Cassie, moving out of the teacher's little room. She still felt a little down. It was the first proper tutu she had ever owned and it would never be the same again.

Becky still looked guilty and worried when Cassie got back to the girls' dressing-room. She had bought some nougat the day before and insisted that Cassie had it all, to make amends.

'I don't want it, Becky!' she argued.

'Oh, please have it. It'll make me feel so much better if you do!'

'I'll have it if it's going begging,' piped up Rhiannon cheekily.

'Oh all right then,' said Cassie, seeing Becky's expression. 'I'll have the nougat. I'll end up sharing it out anyway.'

'Oh yum!' said Rhiannon.

Fragments of the music from the French school's ballet came floating down to the dressing-room, indicating that the programme had begun.

'Oh, I'm so glad we're not first on tonight,' said Cassie.

'I don't know,' said Jane. 'This way, you have more time to get nervous.'

But Poppy had thought of that; she produced a pack of cards, which provided entertainment for the next hour.

Cassie waited outside her dressing-room, to catch Claudette as she came offstage at the end of *La Fille Mal Gardée*.

'How did it go?' she asked, when she saw her.

'Bien,' Claudette answered. 'Very well, I think. Good luck for you!'

'Thanks,' said Cassie.

During the interval, all the English girls were getting decidedly nervous. Cassie's newly-acquired nougat came in very useful.

Then it was time for their ballet to begin. They were presenting a shortened version, to fit it into just one half.

'Good luck,' called Madame, as the beginners made their way past her into the wings.

Cinderella went very well. All the fairies' solos were well received and Cassie felt pleased with her own dancing. Madame gave Cassie permission to stay in the wings to watch the ball scene.

The Ugly Sisters seemed better than ever. Their dances with the courtiers were hilariously funny. By contrast, the pas de deux of the Prince and Cinderella was lyrical and charming.

Ojo seemed to excel himself in the leaping section of the dance. Cassie had never seen him jump so high. But then came disaster! Ojo was flying round the stage, turning and leaping, when he misjudged the distance, stumbled heavily and nearly slipped into the orchestra pit.

Dancers, like skaters, are used to having tumbles and just picking themselves up and getting on with it, but when Ojo tried to do that, he found his right leg collapsed when he put any weight on it.

The curtains were quickly closed and Ojo helped off stage. Members of the ballet staff appeared from nowhere. By now, Ojo was crying with pain. Matthew and Abigail tried to comfort him as best they could. Cassie was sent to find Mr Whistler.

Miss Waters thought he had either torn a ligament or sustained a fracture. She advised Mr Whistler to take Ojo off to hospital immediately.

Cassie wondered if they would be able to finish the ballet after this crisis, but then she noticed Madame talking earnestly to Tom. When Madame went off to make an announcement, Cassie ran over to him.

'Are you dancing the Prince?' she asked.

'Yes!' answered Tom, eyes wide with fright.

'You'll be fine, don't worry. Do you know where they've got up to?'

'Yes, Madame's just explained. Wish me luck, Cassie. I'm terrified!'

'Best of luck, Tom. Give it all you've got!'

The scene resumed and Tom managed to dance remarkably smoothly. As Cassie watched from the wings, she felt sure nobody would have guessed how nervous he really was. Abigail helped him through all the joint parts as much as she possibly could.

As he came offstage at the end of the ballet, Cassie and Poppy patted him on the back. 'You were great, Tom!' said Cassie.

Celia and the other Stars followed him off. Celia paused beside them, just as Matthew and Becky joined the group.

'Well done, Tom!' Matthew said. 'That was a brilliant performance!'

Tom smiled bashfully at all the attention he was getting.

'Well, you would say that, Matthew,' Celia broke in. 'You're his friend, after all.'

'I'm only telling the truth,' said Matthew, grinning. He refused to let Celia put him out of temper.

'What rubbish!' Celia cried. 'Tom would have been useless if it hadn't been for Abi. She spoon-fed him all the way through!'

Cassie winced as she saw Tom's expression change; all his confidence drained from him.

'How could you say that?' she shouted indignantly at Celia. 'Don't you care about hurting people's feelings?'

'I just like seeing credit given to the right people, that's all,' said Celia, stalking off with a toss of her head.

'Ooh, that girl,' said Cassie. 'She makes me so mad!'

'Take no notice, Tom,' said Becky. 'You did a marvellous job, believe me.'

'Well, Celia's right, I don't think I could have done it if Abi hadn't been so good at leading me,' said Tom. 'Where is she, anyway?'

'She rushed off to find Madame to see if there was any news of Ojo,' said Cassie.

By the time they returned to the hotel, Abigail had convinced herself that Ojo had been seriously injured. She was very disappointed that he wasn't back from the hospital.

'You always have to wait hours in casualty departments,' said Cassie, 'unless you're dying.'

Cassie, Becky and Poppy started their long haul up to the attic room they were sharing.

'These stairs don't get any easier,' said Becky. 'Just what you need after a hard night on stage!'

As they reached the top of the last flight of steps, Cassie bundled her friends back round the corner.

'I think we have visitors,' she whispered. She motioned them to put their costumes and baggage in a broom cupboard at the top of the stairs.

'Is it the men?' asked Becky in a hushed voice.

'Looks like them,' whispered Cassie. 'They're trying to open our door.'

'What do we do *now*?' hissed Poppy.

'You go down and fetch Madame and the hotel manager, if you can find him,' Cassie whispered. 'We won't let them out of our sight.'

'Right,' said Poppy, 'but don't do anything silly, will you, Cassie?'

'No, of course not!'

Poppy slid noiselessly down the bannister while Cassie and Becky both slipped off their shoes. Becky dared a peep round the corner of the landing.

'They're just going in,' she reported quietly. 'Wait for the booby-trap to go off!'

Their ears strained; they were soon rewarded by the sound of crashing and thudding.

'They've hit the trip-wire,' giggled Cassie excitedly. 'Shall we go in?'

'I don't know,' said Becky, pulling back. 'They might be dangerous. I think we should wait for Madame.'

'They won't be dangerous with two piles of chairs on top of them, will they?' scoffed Cassie.

Their booby-trap had been made by running a length of string between two teetering stacks of chairs, just inside the door. Once the string had been tripped over, the chairs were stacked in such a way that they would fall inwards, burying the intruders.

'Come on, Becky. Don't be wimpish.'

Becky took a deep breath. 'OK,' she said. 'I'm right behind you.'

They marched along the landing and into their room, feeling like arresting policeman. The man who had worn the beret in Amiens, and who still wore a stripy jumper, was sitting on the floor looking dazed, amid a jumble of chairs. The man with the scar, however, was already on his feet and facing the door.

'Allez, allez!' he shouted at the girls, gesturing them aside. He pulled his accomplice onto his feet and shouted something to him. He spoke too quickly for the girls to understand.

'I'm not budging,' Cassie said to Becky, thrusting out her chin, 'until Madame arrives with the hotel manager.'

Becky looked unsure. The scar-faced man's eyes

were darting all over the room. Suddenly he plunged towards Becky's bed and seized Teddy Pierre. Gabbling to the other man, he came towards the girls.

Cassie steeled herself to bar their way, but the men pushed her roughly aside. As they barged out on to the landing, Cassie quickly recovered her balance. She darted after them and grabbed the teddy from the man with the scar. She took him by surprise and got the teddy clean out of his grip. He turned, furious, and lunged towards her.

At that moment, Poppy rounded the corner from the stairs with Madame, Mr Whistler and the hotel manager. The men looked round and knocked the girls out of the way, snatching back Teddy Pierre as they did so. They hared off down the corridor.

Becky stayed on the floor, winded. Cassie led the others down the corridor in pursuit of the men.

'They can't escape,' said Poppy. 'We've cut off the way to the stairs.'

But, between gasps, the overweight manager was saying something to Madame.

'The skylight!' she cried.

They all put on a spurt, but the men had a head start. The pursuers were in time to see the last pair of legs vanishing up through the skylight. Mr Whistler made a vain attempt at hanging onto the man's feet, but only succeeded in pulling one of his shoes off.

The manager then gave Mr Whistler a leg up. He

pulled himself up athletically through the open skylight.

'Pity Becky missed that!' said Poppy, as he disappeared.

But Cassie was already moving forward. 'Give me a leg up, Poppy,' she ordered.

'And where do you think you're going, young lady?' asked Madame.

'Onto the roof!' said Cassie, as if it were the most natural thing in the world.

'Oh no, you don't,' said Madame.

By this time, the sound of police sirens could be heard, rising from the street below.

'Oh, I wonder what's happening?' cried Cassie. 'Shouldn't I go and see if Mr Whistler's all right?'

As if in reply, Mr Whistler's feet and legs came dangling through the skylight. He jumped down lightly onto the landing. Cassie hadn't noticed Becky coming up behind her.

'Oh isn't he agile?' she whispered adoringly in Cassie's ear.

'Are you all right, Becky?'

'Yes, fine. What's been . . . ?'

'Shh,' warned Cassie. She didn't want to miss what Mr Whistler was saying.

' . . . got away, I'm afraid. They jumped over to another roof. It didn't feel too safe up there, so I left it to the police. The street seems to be swarming with them.'

Once Madame had translated all this to the

manager, the three adults hurried off downstairs. They took one piece of evidence with them: the shoe.

'That's a bit of luck,' said Cassie. 'We can go and clear up the chairs and no one will be any the wiser!'

'I hope the police catch them,' said Becky. 'I wonder when we'll find out.'

'Well, instead of just hanging around, wondering, why don't we go and see?' suggested Cassie.

Her friends started to move towards the stairs.

'No, not that way!' cried Cassie. 'We won't see much from the ground. Let's have a look from the skylight.'

'But, Cassie,' Becky protested, 'Madame said you weren't allowed on the roof.'

'Oh, we won't go onto the roof,' Cassie said persuasively. 'Just poke our heads through the skylight, that's all!'

Becky and Poppy looked at one another, but curiosity got the better of them. With a leg up from Becky, Cassie hauled herself up to sit on the frame of the window, but Becky and Poppy were content to fetch a chair to stand on.

They were just in time to see two shadowy figures leaping across another gap between roofs, to another hotel. They disappeared, probably into the building, Cassie thought. Two policemen came up onto an adjoining roof-top, but they had lost the men.

'Oh no,' groaned Cassie, 'I think they've given the policemen the slip.'

'Don't worry, Cassie,' said Poppy, 'they've got to come out into the street sometime, and look at the number of police waiting for them down there!'

'I just have a horrible feeling they're going to get away.'

The girls let themselves down again into the landing and ran back to their room, to start tidying up.

'At least we know now what they were looking for,' said Cassie, retrieving Teddy Edouard from the broom cupboard, along with her costume. She stared at him intently. 'What secret do you have hidden inside you?' she asked.

'I wish they hadn't taken my teddy,' said Becky. 'I'd only just bought him.'

'And won't they be mad when they discover they've got the wrong one!' cried Poppy.

'Whatever has been hidden inside Teddy Edouard must be worth a lot of money,' said Becky, 'or they wouldn't have bothered following us all over the place!'

Cassie started to laugh.

'What's funny?' asked Poppy.

'I was just thinking about the bucket of water trap. It must have been them who sprung it.'

Becky and Poppy saw the joke. 'They must have been soaked!' said Becky, giggling.

'Should we cut your teddy open?' asked Poppy, when they'd stopped laughing.

'Not yet,' said Cassie. 'Let's get these chairs taken

back. I've a feeling we'll have a visit from the police before too long.'

'Oh yes,' said Becky. 'They're bound to ask us for their descriptions. We're the only ones who saw them properly.'

'I don't think the others will have noticed them taking your teddy, Becky,' Cassie went on. 'It all happened so quickly.'

'Does that matter?'

'Yes. I want you to keep it quiet,' Cassie answered, 'at least until we've had a good look at Teddy Edouard. Otherwise, they'll confiscate him, won't they?'

The other two agreed to keep Teddy Pierre's kidnapping to themselves. By the time the police arrived with Madame, the girls were sitting in a completely tidy room, innocently playing cards.

A young, dark-haired man in a white raincoat, obviously a detective, asked them questions in precise English. They were careful to answer as truthfully as possible, describing their first encounter with the men from Amiens and all the subsequent sightings of them. But they didn't mention the teddy-bears at all, either the purchase of Teddy Edouard, or the kidnapping of Teddy Pierre.

The detective stood up at the end of the interview and smiled. He was very handsome, Cassie thought, when he smiled.

'Don't worry,' he said. 'We'll catch them. If not tonight, then very soon.'

'What a night!' Cassie exclaimed as the door shut behind the policemen. 'I'm too wound up to sleep.'

'Oh I don't know,' said Becky, yawning. 'I think I could fall asleep on a log.'

Cassie went over to the small dormer window and drew back one of the curtains. 'It's funny to think those two are out there somewhere. There are still quite a few police cars in the street. I do hope they catch them tonight!'

10

Poor Teddy Edouard

Ojo was livid that he'd missed all the excitement of the night before. He hadn't got back to his room until nearly four in the morning, by which time all was quiet in the hotel.

When Cassie saw Ojo at breakfast, he was sitting with his right leg strapped up and resting on another chair.

'Just my luck,' he protested to Abigail, Tom and Matthew. 'Not only do I lose my chance to dance in the rest of the tour, but I miss out on all the action too!'

'We didn't see much,' said Matthew. 'It was Cassie and Becky who were in the thick of it.'

'And me!' broke in Poppy.

'I'm glad that we at least had a hand in setting up the booby-trap,' said Tom. 'I'd have given anything to see their faces when the chairs fell on their heads.'

'The one crook looked quite wobbly,' said Becky, 'but the other must have had a very hard head.'

'The one with the scar, do you mean?' asked Poppy.

'Yes, he's the fiercest, by far,' said Cassie.

'He was the one who stole my—' Becky clapped her hand to her mouth and looked guiltily at Cassie.

'I didn't know anything had been stolen,' said Matthew, looking interested.

'We haven't told the police,' Cassie whispered. 'You'll have to be sworn to secrecy.'

'I swear,' said the boys together.

'So do I,' said Abigail.

'Well, they've taken Becky's new teddy, mistaking him for mine, we think.'

'Did you buy yours from the shop in Amiens?' asked Ojo.

'That's right,' said Cassie. 'There's something in him they want back.'

'Have you investigated?' asked Abigail.

'No, I need some sharp scissors to cut him open,' Cassie answered.

'I've got some,' said Abigail. 'You can have them after breakfast.'

'Great. Thanks.'

'Do you think the police will have nabbed them yet?' asked Tom.

118

'Not so far,' said Cassie. 'I asked Madame a bit earlier, and she said there was no news of an arrest. Disappointing isn't it!'

'Not as disappointing as not being able to dance for the rest of the tour!' moaned Ojo.

'At least it wasn't a fracture,' Abigail consoled him.

'I know, but torn ligaments take weeks to heal,' said Ojo miserably.

'There are only two performances to go,' said Cassie, 'and it's not as if we can't manage without you.'

As soon as she had spoken, she knew it wasn't the most tactful thing to say, but luckily Ojo didn't take it amiss.

'No, Tom got through it fine,' said Abigail. 'Though I don't think we make such a handsome couple.'

Ojo flashed her a brilliant smile.

'Stop worrying, Ojo,' said Cassie. 'Just sit back and relax. You could really enjoy the next few days in Arras. Have a real holiday.'

'Yes,' said Matthew. 'Get the girls fetching and carrying for you!'

Cassie pretended to take a swipe at him. She was pleased to see Ojo looking a good deal happier.

After breakfast, Cassie called in at Abigail's room to borrow her scissors. She thought Celia looked suspicious.

'What are those for?' she asked.

'Nothing much,' answered Cassie, rushing off

before she had chance to ask her anything else.

Back in the attic room, Poppy and Becky were packing hurriedly. Cassie lay Teddy Edouard on the bed.

'You'd better get a move on, Cassie,' Becky warned. 'Our time in Paris is nearly over!'

'Let's just hope those two villains don't follow us to Arras as well,' said Poppy.

'At least the police are going to guard our new hotel and the stage door,' said Cassie.

'Are they?'

'Yes, Madame told me this morning. She said we needn't worry any more about them. The police will protect us.'

'I hope she's right,' said Becky with a shudder.

Cassie had cut a slit down Teddy Edouard's back and was pulling out handfuls of stuffing.

'I hate doing this to you,' she murmured.

'Found anything yet?' asked Poppy.

Cassie shook her head. She continued to cut up through her teddy's head and took every last bit of stuffing out of him.

'No, nothing here,' she said. 'I don't know if I'm disappointed or relieved.'

The other two came over to help sift through the stuffing, but their search drew a blank.

'It's baffling,' said Becky. 'Why on earth did they want the teddy then? You don't think they just took it out of spite, do you?'

'I don't know,' said Cassie. 'The whole thing's a

total mystery. Unless – perhaps they were looking for your money-box.' She fixed Becky with her eyes.

'Oh go on, then,' said Becky, sighing. 'I know you won't be happy until you've seen what's inside.'

'The only way in is to crack it, I'm afraid,' said Cassie, after studying the money-box.

Before Becky could change her mind, she brought the heel of her shoe down on it sharply, breaking the plastic. She was able to pull it into two halves, revealing a French bank-note in its secret compartment.

'Oh look!' cried Becky, seizing the note. 'How much is it worth?' she asked excitedly. But her face fell when she recognised it as one of her own ten-franc notes.

'Sorry, Becky,' said Cassie, picking up the ruined money-box. 'It was the only way to be sure, though.'

'Oh well,' said Becky ruefully. 'At least I'm ten francs better off than I thought I was.'

There was a knock on the door. Cassie started to hide the rather sad-looking remains of Teddy Edouard, but Celia walked in before she'd finished.

'That's a strange thing to be doing to your teddy-bear!' she said, having a good look. 'I suppose that's why you wanted Abi's scissors. I've come for them, so she can pack them in her suitcase.'

Cassie gritted her teeth and handed over the scissors. She very much doubted that Abigail had sent Celia on such an errand, but thought it best to say nothing.

'Well done, Cassie,' said Becky, once Celia had gone. 'I was expecting an outburst!'

Becky and Poppy helped Cassie to pack her things, and very soon they were all sitting on the coach on their way to Arras.

'Did you see the police car by the hotel entrance?' asked Matthew, leaning across the aisle.

'Yes, we saw it,' said Cassie. 'I just wish it would escort us to Arras.'

The girls spent most of the journey scrutinising faces in the cars following the coach.

'I don't think they'd be so obvious,' said Matthew, when he realised what they were doing.

'No,' agreed Cassie with a sigh. 'I'd love to know how they've been tracking us so far!'

Cassie had dozed off by the time they reached their destination. She tumbled out of the coach and into their new hotel, only half-awake. It was a much smaller establishment than the hotel in Paris and had a friendly, homely air about it. Cassie was pleased to be sharing with Becky and Poppy but, as it was a bigger room, they were also to share with Abigail and Celia.

Cassie's heart sank. She disliked Celia's company at the best of times, but now, in the middle of this mystery, she could hardly bear the thought of Celia's presence. Added to that, Abigail and Celia were still not on good terms.

The five girls unpacked in an uneasy atmosphere.

'Are we doing any sightseeing in Arras?' asked

Becky, to lighten the mood.

'Don't think we'll get time for much,' Cassie answered. 'After all we're only here for one night.'

'And we've got a rehearsal and a performance to fit in,' added Poppy, looking at her watch. 'In fact, we've got to go down to the Town Hall in a minute!'

Cassie fished Teddy Edouard's skin and stuffing out of her case. He looked a sorry sight. She sighed.

'I suppose I haven't time to sew him up now.'

'Not really,' Poppy agreed.

'Whatever did you cut him up for?' Celia cried. 'Was it in one of your tempers?'

'Certainly not,' Cassie snapped, but her tone didn't deter Celia.

'Or were you looking for something?' she asked, with a shrewd look.

This came a bit too close for Cassie's liking. 'For heaven's sake, mind your own business!' she shouted. 'If you don't get off my back I'll . . . I'll . . .'

'Yes?' prompted Celia. 'You'll what?'

'I don't know!' admitted Cassie in exasperation, 'but I'll think of something.'

Fortunately, at that moment the girls were called down to the entrance lobby.

'You'll need your practice clothes and a raincoat,' said Miss Waters, who had brought the message. 'It's just started to rain.'

'Aren't we going by coach?' asked Abigail.

'No,' said Miss Waters, with a smile. 'The Town Hall's only just round the corner.'

Cassie's spirits revived during the short walk to the Town Hall, especially when she saw the policeman guarding the hotel entrance.

As they came into the Town Hall, they were staggered by the two giant figures which greeted them. They were effigies which were used in the town's annual procession.

'Wow!' said Becky. 'Must be bigger than the B.F.G.!'

The girls were shown to a large communal dressing-room, where they quickly donned their leotards, tights and ballet shoes.

'My hair's a mess this morning,' Cassie complained, looking at her reflection. No matter how much hairspray she used, she couldn't stop wisps of hair escaping from her pinned-up plaits.

'Watch out for Miss Oakland,' said Poppy. 'She's taking class and rehearsal this morning. They say Madame's not feeling well.'

'Poor Madame!' cried Cassie. 'She must have been worrying about the intruders!'

The friends hoped that Miss Oakland would make allowances for the fact that they had had a very disturbed and eventful night, but it soon became obvious that she was her usual exacting self.

She pounced on Cassie almost immediately.

'Just because we're in a different country doesn't mean to say you're allowed to let our Redwood standards slip,' she said. 'Your hair is most untidy, Cassandra. Please return to the changing-room and correct it.'

Cassie curtseyed and hurried off. She seized Becky's pot of hair gel and doused her hair liberally with it before re-plaiting.

When she returned to the stage, the class had moved on to the adage section and Cassie was able to take this opportunity to calm her frayed nerves. Dancing nearly always made her feel better.

Class over, the girls made way for the boys to have their ballet class with Mr Whistler. Ballet didn't come quite as naturally as tap dancing to Mr Whistler. The boys were already very well-schooled however and knew exactly what they had to practise.

Miss Waters handed out lunch-packs, provided by the hotel, to the girls in their dressing-rooms.

'You might as well be eating these while the boys are on stage,' she suggested.

Ojo, who was fed up with watching the boys' class, hobbled into the girls' changing-room and made himself comfortable. After offers of sandwiches and nibbles, he settled down to an early lunch.

'At least I shall eat well today,' he said, looking brighter. 'I'll have my second lunch with the boys.'

Abigail laughed. 'Your appetite is obviously fine, how's the leg?' she asked.

Ojo winced in reply. He was beginning to enjoy receiving so much sympathy.

While the boys had their lunch-break, the girls were allowed to go up the seventy-five metres tall Town Hall belfry.

'Thank goodness there's a lift,' said Becky as she,

Cassie, Rhiannon and Poppy got into it.

'Sounds a bit creaky,' said Poppy. 'Hope it doesn't get stuck halfway up.'

When they got out of the lift, the girls were greeted by over thirty winding steps. Becky groaned.

'Come on, Becky,' Cassie called over her shoulder, 'all that lunch should have given you some energy.'

'We're pretty high up!' exclaimed Rhiannon, as they emerged at the top of the belfry. 'And look at this enormous bell!'

'Not as high as the Eiffel Tower, thank goodness,' said Becky.

The girls gazed down upon the town, spread below them like a three-dimensional map.

'I wonder if the two men are down there somewhere,' Cassie said suddenly.

'I doubt it,' said Poppy. 'Even if they haven't already been caught, the police presence will put them off following us, I'm sure.'

When they got back down, Cassie retired into the wings, as the principals began the ballet, and stood watching, next to Tom.

'How are you feeling now about dancing the Prince?' asked Cassie.

'Still nervous,' said Tom. 'I've got the whole thing to do tonight, not just the last bit.'

'Well at least you've got this rehearsal.'

'Yes, thank goodness. It's my memory that worries me. I really don't know all the dances by heart.'

'When you hear the music and see what Abi's

doing, you'll remember,' said Cassie.

'I certainly hope so,' said Tom.

Cassie was surprised to see Madame come into the wings. She curtseyed and Tom bowed to her.

'Are you feeling better now, Madame?' she asked.

'Yes thank you, Cassandra. A little. And 'ow about you? It must 'ave been a frightening experience for you last night.'

'Oh, I'm fine,' said Cassie, 'just rather tired.'

'Yes,' said Madame looking worried. 'It is too much strain on you girls. I feel thankful we 'ave only one more performance after tonight.'

'Any news from the police?' asked Cassie.

'I've just phoned them from the hotel. Still no luck, I'm afraid!'

Under her confident exterior, Cassie felt a little tremor of fear.

Once the rehearsal was under way, however, all thoughts about the men from Amiens were forgotten. Miss Oakland whipped through the first act, at breakneck speed, but went through the scenes involving the Prince in a slow and methodical manner, so that Tom had plenty of opportunity to learn his part.

The rehearsal took longer than usual and, when the students returned to the hotel, they were late for tea. They had only a brief rest after their meal before it was time to get their costumes ready for the short walk back to the Town Hall.

It was still raining.

'Well this isn't very spring-like,' Becky grumbled as they avoided puddles on the pavement.

'I feel sorry for our police guards,' said Cassie, 'having to stand out in this!'

Another police officer had been stationed outside the Town Hall, next to the stage entrance.

'Makes you feel safer, doesn't it!' said Poppy, as they walked past him and through the door.

'Good luck!' Cassie called to Tom, as he and the boys headed off for their dressing-room.

'Thanks, I need it!' Tom called back.

Act One went very smoothly. As the fairies came off into the wings, led by Poppy, Madame congratulated them all.

'That was the best yet!' she exclaimed.

Cassie rushed off to borrow a needle and thread from Miss Waters. She took them back to the dressing-room and fished the remains of Teddy Edouard out of her bag.

'Good job Celia's on stage,' Poppy remarked, 'or we'd be in for another row.'

Cassie thrust the stuffing back into the bear and started sewing up the back seam. Rhiannon came over to inspect it.

'I can see you don't do much sewing,' she said.

'Only darning ballet shoes,' said Cassie.

'Here, let me do it for you,' she offered.

Cassie gladly let Rhiannon take over. She made a much neater job of it than Cassie would have done.

'I think I'm going to sneak up into the wings to

see how Tom's getting on,' said Cassie, when Teddy Edouard was looking more his old self, though not quite so evenly plump.

She got to the wings in time for one of the main pas de deux between Cinderella and the Prince. Tom seemed to be coping admirably. Then came Abigail's solo. Tom walked to the back corner, right next to where Cassie was standing, to await his own solo. He saw Cassie and whispered out of the corner of his mouth, 'What do I do next? My mind's gone a complete blank.'

Cassie's mind raced. 'You start with those two assemblés, you know, ending in a lunge after the second. Then – umm – it's the sissones and pirouettes, and—'

But already Abigail's solo had finished and the applause was dying away.

'There's no more time, Tom,' Cassie hissed. 'Just improvise! Good luck!'

Tom's expression of panic disappeared as he stepped forward during the opening bars of his music. His face automatically assumed a smile as he followed Cassie's instructions in his head.

Cassie watched like a hawk. After the pirouettes anything could happen. But his smile became more relaxed and Cassie realised with great relief, that he'd remembered the rest of his solo.

'That was nerve-wracking,' she said to Poppy, who had joined her in the wings. 'It's so awful for understudies when they have to step in suddenly.'

'Well at least it won't happen to you,' said Poppy. 'We've only got the show in Boulogne tomorrow night and that's it!'

11

Hide and Seek

'I'm glad you got through the rest of the show OK,'
Cassie told Tom the next morning at breakfast. 'You
looked terrified when you told me you'd forgotten
your solo!'

'I was terrified!' Tom answered.

'I could get used to doing nothing,' said Ojo,
munching a croissant with his feet up on a chair. 'In
fact, it feels as if I'm really on holiday.'

'We could do with a bit of a break,' said Cassie.
'I'm shattered.'

There was a welcome announcement from Madame
in the dining-room.

'I 'ave cancelled the rehearsal in Boulogne today, to give you a little more time for relaxation.'

A cheer went up, much to the amusement of the other few hotel guests.

The coach was to leave Arras at nine o'clock sharp, so the girls had to do some hurried packing.

'The tour seems to be going by so quickly now,' said Poppy, laying her beautiful white Fairy Godmother costume in her case.

'I know,' Cassie agreed. 'I can't believe it's Friday already.'

'I'm looking forward to going home now,' said Becky. 'I'm fed up with mystery men!'

'Well, we didn't see them yesterday,' said Cassie. 'The police must have put them off. Pity really.'

'What!' Becky exploded.

'I mean it's a pity that we may never find out what they were looking for.'

'Well, I'm quite happy not to know,' said Becky, 'as long as they leave us alone.'

By lunch-time, they were settled into the new hotel on the outskirts of Boulogne, ready for their last afternoon and night in France.

'Ooh, this is comfy,' said Becky, bouncing up and down on her bed.

'Watch it,' warned Poppy. 'It's an old building. The floor might cave in.'

After a tasty lunch, they were split into groups for sightseeing. The friends were put in Mr Whistler's group – to Becky's delight. The coach took them into the city centre.

They drove through a drab area of modern concrete garages and warehouses. But the fishing and ferry port looked much more lively.

The coach came to a halt outside a massive gate in a tall and very ancient-looking wall.

'These ramparts go right round the old part of the town,' explained Mr Whistler. He arranged with the coach driver, Frank, to pick them up again at four o'clock.

'That's a nice teddy you've got there,' Frank said gruffly, as Cassie passed his cab.

'Oh thanks,' said Cassie, surprised he was being pleasant for a change.

Inside the town walls, it was like going back in time. The friends picked their way along little cobbled streets. Wherever they walked, the enormous domed cathedral loomed over them.

'What's the cathedral called?' Becky shyly asked Mr Whistler.

'Notre Dame,' he answered. 'Madame said it had a labyrinth of passages and rooms underneath it and even the remains of a very old Roman temple.'

'Can we go round it?' she asked.

'Later,' said the teacher. 'I wanted to show you the market first.'

'Have you noticed how all the cathedrals we've seen are called Notre Dame?' Cassie remarked to Becky, as they followed Mr Whistler to the large

open-air market. Rabbits, poultry, herbs, goats'
cheeses, lettuces, wild mushrooms and posies of
flowers were being offered for sale.

The market teemed with people. Becky pulled
Cassie over to look at a stall where live rabbits and
ducklings were on display.

'Aren't they darlings?' she cried, looking at the tiny
yellow ducklings. 'It's funny how their feet always
look too big for them at that age.'

The stall-holder invited Becky to hold one. After
her, Cassie took the warm, feathery bundle into her
hands, feeling the tiny heart beating against her
fingers. She sneezed and Becky hurriedly took the
duckling away again.

'The rabbits are gorgeous too,' said Becky
adoringly. 'Which one do you like best?'

Cassie considered each one carefully.

'The black and white one with floppy ears, I think.'

'They're called lop-eared rabbits,' said Becky. 'I've
always fancied one myself.'

Cassie laughed. 'To add to your zoo!' She looked
round. 'Where are the others?'

'Didn't notice them moving off,' said Becky, also
looking about her. 'It's so difficult to see in this
crowd.'

'I expect we'll bump into them again before long,'
said Cassie.

They wandered round the market, looking at the
stalls, but they didn't come across Mr Whistler and
the rest of the group.

'Do you think they'll have missed us by now?' said Becky, starting to feel worried.

'It's hopeless trying to find anyone in this market,' said Cassie. 'Let's go to the cathedral. I think we've more chances of meeting up with them there.'

They passed pavement cafés where many people were sitting, enjoying the early afternoon sunshine, and entered the hushed, darker atmosphere of the cathedral.

'Wow, it's so peaceful in here after the market!' Becky whispered.

Despite the number of tourists moving round it, there was a feeling of vast, empty space. The girls followed a route round the outside of the cathedral, looking at marble tombs, dignified statues and vast paintings. They kept half an eye open for Mr Whistler.

In the central chapel the girls stopped in front of a lovely wooden statue of the Virgin Mary.

'Look at her crown,' whispered Cassie, in awe. 'It's studded with real gems.'

'Yes, I think you're right,' said Becky, looking more closely. 'Isn't it beautiful?'

Cassie stiffened suddenly. Two men had just come into the chapel. Although their faces were in shadow, Cassie recognised them instantly. She cast around for an escape route.

'Come quickly,' she hissed to Becky, pulling at her sleeve. 'The men from Amiens!'

As they hurried to the exit on the other side of the

chapel, Cassie was very conscious of Teddy Edouard poking his head out of the top of her shopping bag. *They must still be after him,* she thought. *But why?*

Emerging from the chapel, Cassie glanced behind her. The men were following. How could she lose them?

She noticed a sign pointing down a flight of steps, indicating the crypt and cellars.

'Down here,' she said to Becky. They fled down the steps and turned into a long passageway. Fortunately, there were many other passages leading off it, to either side. The only problem was that they were roped off. The public were meant to go straight ahead to the eleventh century crypt. This didn't deter Cassie. She leaped over one of the ropes on the left, quickly followed by Becky.

The twists and turns of this side passage meant they were safely out of sight before the men had come down the steps. The girls paused to listen. Their footsteps echoed down the main passageway.

'They've probably gone to the crypt,' said Cassie quietly.

'What do we do now?' asked Becky. 'Explore?'

It seemed better to keep moving somehow, even though they had no idea where the tunnel would lead them. They passed a series of small cell-like rooms and joined up with another passage.

Voices ahead alerted them to the fact that they were very near to the crypt. Cassie dared a peep round the last bend of the passage. She drew her head back and flattened herself against the wall. Then, slowly and silently, she and Becky moved back along the tunnel until they were safely out of earshot.

'Were they there?' whispered Becky.

'Yes,' Cassie answered. 'They'd come out of the crypt and were going down a tunnel on the other side of the main passageway.'

'Oh no!' exclaimed Becky. 'They'll probably explore all the passages. I'm scared, Cassie. Shall we get out of here while they're out of the way?'

'No, it's too risky,' said Cassie, 'especially as we might not find the others. We must find somewhere to hide down here till they get fed up.'

'What about the crypt?' Becky suggested. 'They've already looked there.'

'No, if they came back, we'd be cornered,' said Cassie. 'There's only one way in or out. No, we'd better go down another passage and look for a good hiding place.'

Becky grimaced. 'But that means coming out into the main passageway again!'

'No, if you remember, two passages joined back there. Let's retrace our steps and go down the other branch.'

'Let's just hope those two don't choose this one to explore next!' Becky exclaimed, with a shiver.

After following the winding passage for some way, the girls came across the perfect hiding-place. In a small recess, stood a large black tomb. They wriggled behind it.

'It's a good job we're slim,' breathed Cassie.

'How long do you think we'll have to stay here?' asked Becky, developing pins and needles in one leg very quickly.

Cassie peered at her watch. 'A while yet. I think we should wait until just before four o'clock, then make a run for it. At least we know where the coach will be then.'

'You think of everything,' said Becky. Cassie couldn't tell if she was being sarcastic.

'Got a better plan?' Cassie asked.

'Well no,' Becky admitted.

The minutes ticked by very slowly. Becky's pins and needles seemed to have spread to every limb. 'Oooh,' she moaned.

'Contract and relax the muscles in your feet and legs rhythmically,' said Cassie. 'Imagine you're dancing – it really works.'

'Pooh,' said Becky, but after trying it for a few minutes, she had to admit it did the trick.

'Can we go yet?' she whispered.

Cassie consulted her watch again. 'Yes, I reckon we can. They must have given up by now, surely.'

As they prepared to move out, some sixth sense warned Cassie to stay put. She pulled Becky back down beside her and put her finger on Becky's lips. Now, faint footsteps could be heard, getting closer and louder as they came towards them. Cassie could feel Becky beginning to tremble against her. It was the men all right, she was sure of it now. She could hear them talking as they approached the recess.

Oh, walk straight past! Cassie willed them.

Instead, the footsteps stopped just level with the tomb. Cassie heard the sound of a lighter being used, and smelled smoke as the men lit up cigarettes. She caught a snatch of their conversation.

' . . . *trop tard* . . .' *That means too late,* she thought. Perhaps they were about to give up the search?

Get moving! Cassie ordered them, mentally.

To the girls' great relief, the men quickly walked off down the tunnel. Even so, Cassie and Becky didn't dare move for another ten minutes.

'We'd better go now,' whispered Cassie. 'I just hope the coach has waited for us.'

'What if they're still about?' Becky hissed.

'We'll have to risk it,' said Cassie. 'Ready?'

They removed their shoes, stuffing them alongside Teddy Edouard in Cassie's shopping bag and ran soundlessly through the winding labyrinth. Fortunately, they didn't lose their way, and emerged at the foot of the steps. They glanced back along the main passage, but there was no sign of the men; so they put their shoes back on and raced up the steps back to the main part of the cathedral.

'We're in luck, I think,' breathed Cassie as they made their way across the nave. 'They must have gone.'

'Oh what a relief!' sighed Becky, as they emerged into bright daylight and the bustle of the town. They headed quickly for the gate in the town walls where they had been dropped off earlier.

Their hearts lifted when they saw the coach, parked in its previous position.

'Nearly home and dry,' said Cassie.

They sprinted through the gate and waved cheerfully to Frank the driver, as they waited to cross the busy road.

'That's funny,' said Cassie suddenly. 'There's no one else on the coach!' She checked her watch. 'Fifteen minutes past four. They should be here by now.'

'Let's ask Frank,' said Becky.

As they reached the coach, Frank was just putting down his car phone.

'So there you are!' he said. 'They've all been lookin' for you two! Police an' all.'

'Where are the others?' asked Cassie.

'Still lookin',' said Frank. 'Best thing I can do is drive you back to the 'otel and they can tell the police you're safe.'

'Shouldn't we look for Mr Whistler first?' said Becky.

'No, you'll only get lost again,' he said. 'I'll take you back. Then we'll know where you are.'

The girls sank back into the comfortable seats, glad to be on their way back to Madame. Cassie looked out of her window and nearly fell off her seat in surprise.

'There's Abigail and Poppy!' she shrieked. 'Stop the coach, Frank!' she yelled, clambering over Becky and running down to the front of the coach.

'Whatever for?' grumbled Frank, carrying on regardless.

'It's two of our friends,' Cassie yelled. 'Stop, stop!'

'Just two, did you say?'

'Yes, Abi and Poppy. Oh please stop!'

The coach rumbled to a halt and waited while Poppy and Abigail ran down the street towards it. They fell up the steps, gasping, as Frank started the coach up again immediately.

'Steady on, Frank!' cried Abigail.

Frank sped off without answering.

Abigail and Poppy joined their friends and for several minutes there were screeches and exclamations as Cassie and Becky told their story.

'It'll be nice to get back to the hotel,' said Cassie.

'Yes, I'm ravenous,' said Becky. 'Fear always makes me hungry.'

'Anything makes you hungry,' said Cassie. 'I suppose Frank will come straight back for the others.'

'Yes, I guess so,' said Poppy. 'Mr Whistler arranged for all of us to meet up again at the main gate at five. We all split up into twos and threes to look for you.'

'Well we ended up finding you, not the other way round,' said Cassie.

Poppy laughed and looked out of the window. 'I don't remember this road,' she said suddenly.

Cassie and her friends looked out. They were speeding through unfamiliar countryside. An uneasy feeling came over Cassie and two memories came sharply into focus.

One was Frank complimenting Teddy Edouard. The other was him speaking on the car phone, when he first saw Cassie and Becky outside the main gate.

She rushed to the back of the coach and looked out of the rear window. A black car was following, with darkened windows, so you could not see who was driving.

She went back to her friends with a stricken expression.

'I think we've been trapped!' she said.

12

Surprises for Cassie

'Frank must be in league with the men,' said Cassie.
'We played right into their hands.'

'And you think it's them behind us?' asked Becky.

'Bound to be, isn't it?' Cassie answered glumly.
'The only thing we can do is try to stop the coach
and make a run for it.'

'But how can we do that?' wailed Becky.

'Well, there's four of us and only one of him,' said
Cassie.

'We might cause an accident,' said Abigail.

'Well, it's either that or sit and wait for Frank to
take us to some hideout of those awful men!' Cassie

exclaimed. 'Come on, let's just do it. Better not to think too hard about it.'

Her heart pounding, Cassie advanced down the aisle, followed by her friends. Before Frank realised what was happening, they had all clambered into the cab and surrounded him. Becky got hold of the handbrake, Cassie grasped the steering wheel and tried to reach with her foot for the brake, while Abigail and Poppy tried to restrain Frank's arms.

Frank kicked Cassie's foot aside and for a perilous few moments, the coach swerved from side to side across the country road, several hands grappling with the steering-wheel.

'What d'yer think yer doing?' shouted Frank.

'Stop! Stop!' Cassie yelled, by now in tears. But Frank wouldn't let Cassie get anywhere near the footbrake. He wrenched the steering-wheel from her; they veered off the road, bumping over the verge. They were heading straight for a tree. Abigail screamed and covered her face.

At last, Frank did an emergency stop, but not in time to avoid collision. He tried to turn the steering-wheel, but was hampered by the girls still clinging to it.

With a sickening jolt, the coach crashed into the tree. Everyone was flung forward, but Cassie, Poppy and Becky managed to hold on to the steering-wheel.

Abigail was not so lucky. She was thrown against the windscreen, banging her head hard. She sank to the floor and lay there without moving.

When they had got over the initial shock, the other three bent over her.

'She's unconscious,' said Cassie. 'We should put her in the recovery position.'

They lifted her gently on to her front, just as Frank let the two men from Amiens on to the coach. The man with the scar was the first on. He counted out a wad of notes and handed them over to Frank.

'Thank you,' said Frank gruffly, 'though I wasn't expectin' all this bother.'

'*Ou est le teddy?*' asked the scar-faced man.

The girls shrank away from him.

'*Le teddy,*' he repeated menacingly.

'In 'er bag,' said Frank, when they didn't reply.

'Bag?' said the man. He moved down the coach, looking for luggage.

'*Voila,*' he said, picking up Cassie's shopping bag. Cassie charged down the coach, too suddenly for the other men to restrain her. The scar-faced man was holding Teddy Edouard. Taking him by surprise, she snatched the toy from him and ran back to her friends.

But there was nowhere else to run. Even if, somehow, they could have got off the coach, they couldn't have left Abigail behind.

Cassie hugged Teddy Edouard tightly to her. The man with the scar advanced down the coach, spouting a torrent of angry French. Above his raised voice, Cassie imagined another noise – a siren. *Wishful thinking!* Cassie thought.

But, no, there really was a siren wailing in the distance. The three men paused and looked round. They had heard it too. All they had to do was jump into their black car and make their escape. How could three schoolgirls stop them?

Cassie's mind raced. She knew how determined they were to get hold of Teddy Edouard, for whatever reason. She gambled on their not leaving without it. All she had to do was to delay them a few more moments. She was sandwiched between the two Frenchmen. They were both moving in. She leaped on to the seat on her right, pulled open the sliding window and hurled Teddy Edouard through it. The men cursed and rushed out of the coach to retrieve it.

Becky and Cassie jumped out onto the damp grass. Frank made no attempt to stop them. Now he had his money, he had no further interest in them. He seemed agitated by the approaching police siren, though. He followed the girls off the coach, hurriedly got into the black car and drove away at high speed, just as the Frenchmen came running back with the teddy-bear.

They looked furious, and started to panic when the police came screeching round the bend and skidded to a halt beside the coach. The men tried to run for it, but three police officers soon had them handcuffed.

Cassie suddenly realised that the fourth policeman was their friendly detective from Paris. He checked that the girls were OK, before radioing for an ambulance for Abigail.

Two of the officers drove the Frenchmen off to the nearest police station, while the other one stayed with Abigail.

'We 'ave been trying to find these two men for a long time,' the young detective explained.

'Even before the break-in at our hotel?' asked Cassie.

'Oh yes, long before that. But we were most puzzled by what they wanted from you.'

He held up Teddy Edouard.

'Did you buy this from the shop where you first saw them?'

Cassie nodded guiltily.

'You should 'ave told us before. You 'ave put yourselves in great danger!'

'But why should they want my teddy?' Cassie burst out.

'These men are gem thieves,' explained the detective. 'I see you 'ave already cut him open.'

'Yes,' said Cassie, 'but there was nothing inside!'

'Mmm, I wonder . . .' mused the detective. He took a penknife from his pocket and gave one of Teddy Edouard's eyes a sharp crack. The plastic split open and he shook out on to the palm of his hand a sparkling white gem.

'A diamond!' cried Cassie, wide-eyed with surprise.

'And I think we may find its partner here,' said the detective, breaking open the other eye. He held out

147

two brilliant diamonds in his hand.

'That's amazing!' said Becky.

'Can I have my teddy back now?' Cassie asked.

The detective shook his head. 'It will have to be examined, I'm afraid.'

'We'd better see how Abi is,' said Cassie. The other police officer was already on the coach with her. Cassie was relieved to see she was sitting up, looking a little dazed, but alert enough to get as excited as Poppy at the news about the diamonds.

'Just think,' said Poppy. 'You've been walking around with two valuable diamonds for days!'

After the ambulance had taken Abigail to hospital, Cassie, Becky and Poppy were driven to the police station, where they made a statement about all that had happened involving the two crooks and Frank.

'Pity the coach driver got away,' said the detective.

'Oh, I was so amazed at seeing the diamonds that I almost forgot to tell you,' said Cassie. 'I memorised the number-plate of the black car.'

He laughed. 'I think we 'ave a lot to thank you for, young lady. It will make up a little for not telling us the 'ole truth in your first interview!'

Cassie blushed deeply. 'Sorry,' she said, 'I just didn't want to lose my teddy.'

The girls came back into the hotel like celebrities. Wherever they went, crowds of fellow students followed them, asking excited questions. But first they had to report to Madame and Mr Whistler to give them the full details. The police had taken Miss Oakland to stay with Abigail during her treatment for concussion.

'How's Abi?' Cassie asked as soon as she could fit a question of her own into the barrage of questions that was coming the girls' way.

'She'll be fine,' answered Madame. 'She's coming out of hospital in the morning. The doctors say she must rest for two or three days, that's all.' She smiled. 'You know what this means, don't you, Cassandra?'

Cassie looked blankly at her. All the excitement of the day had left her rather numb.

'Do you feel up to dancing Cinderella tonight?'

'Tonight?' screeched Cassie.

'If not, we can cancel the show in Boulogne,' said Madame. 'I quite understand if you are too upset by this afternoon's—'

'No, no!' shouted Cassie. 'I'd love to! You mustn't cancel it! But who will do the Spring Fairy?'

'I 'ave already spoken to Celia about it – she is confident she knows it well enough.' Madame beamed at her. 'You are the true professional, Cassandra,' she said affectionately. 'I wish you great success in the role!'

Tea-time and the short rest period which followed seemed to go by in a dream. Cassie mentally rehearsed the dances she would be required to perform that evening. She went to find Tom, to ask him about a few elements of the pas de deux she wasn't sure of.

They marked out the tricky bits together in the corridor.

'It's my turn to be terrified,' said Cassie.

'Yes, it's funny it should be happening to you now,' said Tom. 'I feel like an old hand.'

'You've learned the part of the Prince so well,' agreed Cassie. 'I'm relying on you to steer me through the pas de deux.'

Tom grinned. 'Never thought anyone would rely on *me*,' he said.

Cassie heard Mr Whistler calling everyone to get ready.

'Oh goodness,' said Cassie. 'Where has the time gone? I've got awful butterflies.'

'You'll do it, Cassie, I promise,' said Tom.

As Cassie was zipped into Cinderella's ragged costume, she couldn't believe it was really happening to her. She stood alone on the stage, the curtains still drawn, a hush falling on the audience as the pianist began the overture. Then she knew it was all up to her. The success of their last night depended on her.

Cassie had never concentrated so hard in all her life. The curtains drew back and she began to move round the stage, conscious of the hundreds of pairs of eyes fixed on her and her alone. The theatre seemed enormous. Cassie was relieved when the two Ugly Sisters came bustling on, quarrelling over a silk scarf.

Cassie settled down to her lowly position by the

fire-grate, happy that, for a few minutes at least, the eyes of the audience would be trained on Becky and Matthew, and not on her.

But all too soon, the scarf was ripped and the Ugly Sisters rushed off stage again, still quarrelling. Cassie's heart lurched; now came her first proper solo. She picked up the torn scarf and began a dreamy dance. Cassie had to convince the audience that she was Cinderella desperately wishing she could go to the ball.

Her nerves calmed as she became carried away by the dance. Cassie was Cinderella, and at the end of the dance, she knew she had not let anyone down.

Act One went smoothly, until the transformation of Cinderella by the Fairy Godmother. A lightning change into her ball gown was needed, but Cassie had never practised the change before, and now she had to do it on stage, screened only by the fairies. She was all fingers and thumbs – she would never get it done in the short amount of music allocated to the change! Rhiannon saw her difficulties and gave her a helping hand. Cinderella emerged ready to go to the ball just in time.

The beautiful white gown, the sumptuous golden cloak and sparkling tiara made Cassie feel like a princess for the rest of the ballet. And with Tom as her careful partner, her confidence soared.

If her feet hadn't been aching so much by the end of the ballet, Cassie could have kidded herself that she really had been in a fairy tale. But her three bouquets were real enough – one of them from the young detective from Paris!

Cassie was elated as she stepped forward to take her final curtsey with Tom. It was the very first time she had danced a leading role since joining Redwood Ballet School and she would never forget the experience.

Then it was all over; the last moment of the last performance of the tour. What lay ahead now was a good night's sleep and lots of packing.

Abigail was discharged from hospital the next morning, in time to catch a new coach – driven by a friendly Frenchman – for the ferry port.

Apart from a big bruise on her forehead, Abigail seemed quite well. She plied Cassie with questions about how she'd got on in *Cinderella* the night before.

'I was OK, I think,' said Cassie modestly, 'but it was a pretty nerve-wracking experience!'

'You weren't the only one to go through it,' teased Tom.

'No,' broke in Celia. 'You weren't.'

'Well done, all of you,' said Abigail.

'It was easy-peasy,' said Celia. 'I wasn't even the official understudy for the Spring Fairy, but I managed it.'

Cassie was about to make a retort when Becky trod on her foot.

'Ouch!' said Cassie.

Becky pointed out of the window. The coach was

152

just pulling up into the ferry port.

'What?' asked Cassie, peering out.

'Isn't that our detective?' asked Becky.

'I think it is,' said Cassie. 'Perhaps he's come to wish us *bon voyage*.'

The young detective got on the coach and came down the aisle holding a carrier bag. He thrust the bag towards Cassie.

'Thought you might like this back,' he said. 'And your friend. We made a search of the Amiens shop and look what we found.'

To cries of delight, first Teddy Edouard and then Teddy Pierre were lifted from the bag.

'Oh, thank you!' chorused the girls.

'He's got eyes again!' yelled Cassie in surprise.

The detective grinned. 'We sewed a new pair on for you.'

'Thank you so much,' said Cassie, hugging Teddy Edouard.

'*Bon voyage*,' said the detective.

'*Au revoir*,' said Cassie, smiling.

'If you're thinking of coming back next year,' he said, 'don't buy any more teddies, will you?'

'No,' said Cassie. 'This one got a bit too hot to handle!'